Over the Garden Wall

FINDING MOMENTS THAT MATTER

Debbie Kaiman Tillinghast

Over the Garden Wall: Finding Moments That Matter
Copyright © 2024 Debbie Kaiman Tillinghast

Visit our website at **www.StillwaterPress.com** for more information.

First Stillwater River Publications Edition

ISBN: 978-1-963296-93-8

Library of Congress Control Number: 2024919349

1 2 3 4 5 6 7 8 9 10
Written by Debbie Kaiman Tillinghast.
Cover and interior book design by Matthew St. Jean.
Cover assets by Fresh Stock, egnismoore, artifex.orlova, and weris7554 / Adobe Stock. Spring and summer illustrations by jenesesimre; fall illustration by Viktoriia Holovko / Adobe Stock.
Winter illustration by Elisha Gillette.
Published by Stillwater River Publications,
West Warwick, RI, USA.

Names: Tillinghast, Debbie Kaiman, author.
Title: Over the garden wall : finding moments that matter / Debbie Kaiman Tillinghast.
Description: First Stillwater River Publications edition. | Pawtucket, RI, USA : Stillwater River Publications, [2024]
Identifiers: ISBN: 978-1-963296-93-8 | LCCN: 2024919349
Subjects: LCSH: Gardens--Fiction. | Seasons--Fiction. | Mindfulness (Psychology)--Fiction. | Peace of mind--Fiction. | Well-being--Fiction. | Joy--Fiction. | Grief--Fiction. | LCGFT: Short stories. | Poetry.
Classification: LCC: PS3620.I516 O94 2024 |
DDC: 813/.6--dc23

For my family with all my love.
You have blessed me with countless
moments that matter.

"There are always flowers for those who want to see them."
—*Henri Matisse*

Contents

Spring

I Write Because…	1
The Faithful Gardener	4
Chipmunk Birds and Friends	7
March	9
Where Does Joy Go?	11
Strange Sweet Treat	14
My Lopsided Life	16
Home	19
Open the Door	22
Daffodils in the Woods	24
Holly Cakes	26
The Memory Keeper	28
Spring Bliss	30
The Rocking Chair	33
Daffodil Daze	35
What Do I Value Most?	37
Laila	39
Beyond the Pond	42
A Bittersweet Story	45
May 24	47
Ferry Ride	49
Prelude to Write	52

Summer

Island Summer House	59
My Memory Triggers	62
Fog	65
Rhode Island Summer Generations	67
Friendship	70
The Lady in the Pink Turban	73
I Walk…	76
Growing Anticipation	78
BLT	80
22 Hours	82
Dreams	84
Leaving	85
Treading Water	87
Be Present	89
Summer's Gift	91
Loneliness	93
Alone	95
The Silence Is Alive	96
Listen	99
Healing Notes	101
End of Summer	103
A Day to Write	106

Fall

In Search of Ice Cream	111
Island October	113
Pemaquid Point	115
Autumn Leaves	116

Autumn Gift   119
My Writing Chair   120
Grief   123
Fading Light   126
Words Like Water   127
Grumble or Grateful   129
My Favorite Knife   131
November   134
Laughter   137
A Cactus Story   139
Early Snow   143
Letting Go   145
Lessons from the Ants   148
Thanksgiving Day   150
Blueberry Glue   153
The Dishwasher   156
I Am an Amaryllis   158

Winter

Shortbread Memories   163
Nibble, Nibble Doubt   165
Christmas Circuit Overload   168
Peace   172
Happy New Year   175
Taking Down the Christmas Tree   178
Choices   181
My Lemon Tree   183
Where I Wander   185
Can You See?   188
January Gift   189

Blizzard   191
I Think I Will Remember, But...   194
Soup Days   196
More Than a Meal   198
Moments   200
Coffee and Bluebirds   202
Radiators   204
Winter Music   207
Fickle February   208
Will It Matter?   210
Solitude Shoes   212
Promise Song   215

Recipes   *216*
Acknowledgements   *220*

OVER THE GARDEN WALL

Spring

I Write Because...

Why do I write? I often wonder, but like the kaleidoscope I had as a child, the reasons change with the tiniest movement in my life. I write for joy when I'm happy and to mitigate pain when I'm sad. I write to figure out my life and I write to share its blessings with others. The details in life matter, but we often miss them as we rush headlong through the day. I want to share the dewdrops on the daffodils or the first crocus of spring, the Bluebirds that come to my feeders, and the air on Prudence Island.

I write to capture the world, the yard, the moment, me, on the page. I can share my feelings when no one sits beside me to listen. My soul streams across lined notebook paper in blue or black, pink or lavender, sometimes clear and legible, sometimes disappearing in my scrawny scribble. I preserve moments that I might have lost or ignored—the Phoebe that wakes me on sunny mornings, the winter stillness so different from a quiet summer day, the sound of the wind and the radiators, paper loons circling overhead, oblivious to the person watching them, carried on warm currents of air to another place, another time. I love the tiny moments lost in the cracks of life. The blossom buried under the tent of despair, or the hand of scorn. I write because the moments of joy glisten like raindrops and are as plentiful—if I open my eyes.

Everything passes quickly, like dreams forgotten in an instant. Life goes too fast, writing slows it down, gives time for stillness. I write because I can't stop the snowball from rolling down the hill. It goes faster and faster, on a journey I can't stem, and I realize it always has. I don't want to ride the snowball down, I want to slow it, roll it uphill, not down. I don't want to miss what surrounds me, I want to digest it, make it part of me.

Before, I didn't appreciate the nuances of being present moment to moment, and I missed subtle changes because I didn't pay attention. I searched for release from the pain of a friend's illness, or the death of a loved one, but wandered through the house disconnected from myself, unable to find healing. Now I write my grief on a page; it flows like a lanced boil. I see it, touch it, hear it, and then write myself to clarity and peace.

Writing provides a tether; it brings perspective and care to things I long for in my life. Words appear in unexpected ways and create unforeseen stories. When I can find no place to put myself, words bring definition to my feelings. When my soul feels restless and wanders, searching for a place to be, writing says, "Sit here, hold hands with your own heart, let me be your solace, your resting place, your purpose."

When I finish writing, sometimes teary-eyed, I discover that I found a listening ear when I thought there was none. When I hunger for a tender word, or a hug, but I find emptiness, writing offers an arm and says, "Rest here. I can't change it, but I can share it, I can hold you while you grieve, I can be your soft landing to pillow the hard edges of life."

When I notice the moments, I appreciate the now. When I don't pay attention, and let them slip by, I wonder where days have gone. The moments matter because they provide the foundation of our lives. I listen to the night sounds on a spring evening and am grateful for the stillness that allows the peeper and insect symphony to play in my heart. My hand guides the pen of my soul across the page, and I am alive in this moment, and I am real.

The Faithful Gardener

*G*ardens (both real and metaphorical) require faith and provide food for the soul. I could not put a tiny tomato seed in an egg cup of soil and trust I will be picking tomatoes in a few months, without faith. I could not bury wrinkled brown bulbs eight inches into the ground in the fall and wait patiently for the appearance of bright yellow trumpets in the spring, without faith. I could not stand in the middle of my dry, barren garden in January and anticipate the first purple crocus two months later, without faith.

Gardens reflect the rhythms of life, the order of things: wilting in fall, and dying in winter, only to burst from the earth once more in spring. During the recent years of pandemic sameness, as days rolled by out of control and without direction, one day bleeding into another, a repeat of the one before, I depended on faith. I found comfort in my garden. I watched it unfold, day by day, first one yellow crocus and then clumps of purple scattered about. No matter the capricious swings of weather, warm April days in February or snowstorms that bury the daffodils in April, the garden still has a pattern. The daffodils never bloom before the snowdrops, and a few colorful polka dots in March will grow into a riot of color in the heat of summer, until the last pink chrysanthemum gives in to winter's frosty blanket.

When working in my garden, I soak up peace like crackers in milk; it seeps through my feet and my hands, my nose and my eyes, and my breath calms when I gaze at the blues and pinks—the sea of woodland phlox, the dots of blue forget-me-nots, the shades of pink bleeding hearts.

Even now, I turn to my garden for reassurance; it feeds me with its day-to-day changing colors and smells. Gardening instills patience and demands faith; otherwise, we would give up the first time our hopes and anticipations get thwarted by the weather, the critters, or our own unrealistic expectations. Faith believes without seeing. I believe the temperatures will change, the earth will warm, the rain will fall, and the roses will bloom, even in November, when my desire to sit by the fire surpasses my desire to dig in the dirt. That desire will return on the first warm day of spring. A front yard filled with bright yellow daffodils in April, the wafting aroma of roses in June, and the fragrance of lilies in August feeds my senses, nourishes my eyes, my nose, and my soul with the peace of living things.

People driving by stop and say how much they enjoy seeing my garden evolve each year. They don't say, "It feeds my soul," but I hear the unspoken meaning in their words. The garden nourishes me as I pull weeds or inhale the honey scent of the pink Josie lilacs. I am grateful for the peonies that smell like roses, and the Casa Blanca lilies that perfume my front yard. I am grateful for the tiny crocus that reminds me every year, regardless of how hard the winter is, that spring will come again.

The garden makes the moments matter, makes them real—the fairy dance of the columbine, the butterfly perched on the purple Nepeta—because a year will vanish like a soap bubble unless we notice the moments and hold them close. However bad things may seem in my life, whatever the pain of grief or loneliness I feel, I have faith that I will get through the trials of winter, and I will find spring again.

Chipmunk Birds and Friends

he bite of winter lingers on this early March day, but sharing breakfast with my feathered neighbors cheers me. I savor my coffee in the warmth of a south-facing sunroom window while they gobble their avian treats. Today's snow has brought a flurry of activity, and I am captivated by the birds' quirky personalities as I watch them line up for the daily special. The ceaseless parade begins at sunrise and soon at least fifty birds are vying for a spot, like diners with a punch card they can't wait to fill. The cast changes throughout the day.

An upside-down dining nuthatch arrives first, and he spreads the word, "Breakfast is ready!" Usually the Black-capped Chickadees herald this news, but they must have slept late today. At noon a flock of Goldfinches, dressed in drab winter colors, comes to snack on the thistle seed, while the brilliant red Cardinals favor more tranquil, late afternoon dining. Chickadees and Tufted Titmice stay all day, sampling every feeder, afraid they might miss a tasty morsel; shy Juncos prefer a lower-level table and scavenge on the ground. Two tiny Carolina Wrens arrive and share one block of suet. They dart around my yard in staccato movements. They're jolly little fellows with reddish-brown backs, spiky tails, and white stripes over their beady black eyes. I have renamed them Chipmunk Birds.

Most of my visitors appear content sharing the seed and suet feeders; they occasionally flutter and fluff at each other but then settle down and eat peacefully. Downy Woodpeckers, with one dot of red on the back of their black and white heads, come and go during the day; often two or three occupy one block of suet. The Hairy Woodpecker, larger twin to the Downy, and the Red-bellied Woodpecker dwarf the other birds and have huge beaks that devour large chunks of suet on each visit. In spite of their size, they don't disturb anyone, but graciously share the feeders with the smaller birds, then go on their way. This harmonious dining is only disrupted by the raucous, uncooperative Blue Jays, who stake their territory and allow no one else to intrude. One perches on a branch above the feeders, and every time another bird tries to land, it gets pecked on the head! They are like cranky children who don't want anyone else to play with their toys, even though there are enough for everyone.

The bleak day speeds by and I frequently return to my cozy spot, entranced by the outdoor entertainment. As the snow diminishes and the light begins to fade, I venture outside to restock the breakfast buffet for morning. Two sociable Chickadees stay for a talk. Perched on a branch above my head, they chatter at me.

"Chick-a-dee-dee, where have you been?" When the feeders are full their tone changes.

"Chick-a dee-dee-dee, Chick-a dee-dee-dee," which I translate as,

"Thank you for the yummy food!"

March

March makes me twitchy. It brings a sense of unease, and nothing seems quite right, like sitting on a chair with a spring poking into your back. During my years teaching junior high and high school, I grew restless in March. My patience with the students would temporarily disappear, and I often proclaimed to my colleagues, "I need a new job." I thought this March malaise would end, or at least improve, when I retired, but my soul feels restless, and I am dissatisfied with whatever I'm doing, wherever I am. I refer to it as my March Madness.

Activities that normally soothe, like writing, reading, visiting with friends, or going for a walk, bring no respite from this angst. Although I walk every day, I have to push myself to leave the house. I wonder why I find March walks less fulfilling, and my spirit doesn't lighten as it usually does. Is it the wind that tags along with March in New England? Is it the cold damp that seeps into my bones or the dreary days and colorless world that surround me? Often, snow doesn't soften the barren ground, the plants lie dormant beneath last year's detritus, and the grass lies withered and brown.

One day, aching to find a reason for hope, I walked through cold, dense fog that felt like a frozen cloud. The wind blew a stinging curtain into my face and my gloomy mood matched the gray surrounding me. When I returned to my yard I knelt down and found the first tiny yellow Snow Crocus. I pulled aside a few bits of brittle grass to clear its path to the light. I surveyed the dried remains of winter debris and spotted a few more specks of color that would open in the sun. I found an inch of the green, V-shaped blades of a daffodil pointing through last fall's un-raked leaves, and I imagined the brilliant yellow that would follow.

In that moment my soul found peace. I needed simply to touch the ground and connect with wispy bits of new life to bring balance to my world again. My spirit had been longing for spring and the greening of the earth. Although I still yearned for the soft pink air of April days, I found a tiny spring oasis in my garden and for now, it was enough.

Where Does Joy Go?

Where does Joy go when it leaves us? I wonder, does it exist as a finite living thing that goes on a mission, a heat-seeking missile, searching out a place in need of its infusion? Or does it seek a place where Joy already lives, bringing more because it finds comfort with itself and discomfort when alone? Does it dribble away through an hourglass hole?

Accepting that we are where we belong, and life is as it is meant to be is not always easy. When I wrote *The Ferry Home* and spent time on Prudence Island, joy filled my heart. Writing and Prudence filled my soul. I visited my sons and their wives in Florida, Maryland, and New York. While they worked, I wrote. I didn't feel tied to anything but my stories. I traveled to Maine to visit friends and found peace there too. I volunteered at a meal kitchen once a week, happy to give back. But somewhere, sometime, unnoticed, Joy moved on. I didn't mean for it to leave. Did I do something to force it out, make it uncomfortable in its home within me? I don't know.

My friends fell ill with various life-changing and life-threatening illnesses. I longed to help them, to hold them close, and keep them from sliding down the steep, slippery hill they walked. I wanted to be present, I tried to be supportive—I took soup and cookies, I sat and talked, I listened, but the joy kept trickling away, like a leaky air mattress. The air doesn't leave all at once. You go to sleep with a full, firm bed and wake up to find yourself on the ground. The air has disappeared, the comfort has gone but you didn't see it leave. How do I find Joy and bring it back? Does it hide in my garden with the flowers? Wind within the story I'm writing? Wander somewhere on Prudence? Or does it still live inside me, waiting to be rediscovered?

I visited my son Adam and his family. The worries and pains of home wanted to travel with me—a friend's mental illness, the sorrow of another as she grieves for her husband, the worry for one whose cancer returned. Here, far from home, I briefly set them aside, viewed them with perspective from a distance. Every day holds new adventures, opens the door to different experiences. Adam and I walked on a cool cloudy day. In Tennessee, the daffodils bloomed. The calendar said March but my mind said April. He told me about his work. We had tea, my grandson woke from his nap with a cheerful smile and crawled onto my lap. My heart felt full. Joy trickled back in. The well gradually filled, giving me sustenance for dark days.

Joy can be a fleeting thing; I need to hold it close. There have been times when it flowed abundantly. I didn't think about it all the time, because I had a plentiful supply. But like money, when we have a sufficient amount to meet all our needs, we take it for granted. We waste food, we waste electricity, we sometimes spend foolishly, but when the bank account dwindles, we carefully guard our spending.

Joy has been flowing out of me at an epic rate the last few years—a pandemic, the loss of several longtime friends—I didn't realize it until the well had almost emptied. Now I treasure joyful moments. I don't squander them but hold them close inside, to see me through future distressing times, comforted because I can experience them twice, once in my mind and heart, and once again on the page.

> Joy once lived inside of me,
> I think it still lives there,
> Though I've buried it under a quilt of care.
> Unlock the door, let the sun shine in,
> Joy remains, let the day begin.

Strange Sweet Treat

The sun stretches through the trees and taps me on the shoulder as I sit in my writing chair in the sunroom. Outside, the air remains winter cold, but today it holds the promise of spring. Not warm exactly, but less like winter and the temperature might reach fifty degrees. This temperature swing signals the start of sugaring-off time. The warm days and cold nights push the sap faster and faster, coursing through the maple trees. The farmers harvest sap from the sugar bush—the stand of sugar maples. It drips from taps hammered in the trees, into metal buckets or flexible plastic tubing, then travels to one collection spot.

Sugar houses open for the season with sweet clouds billowing from the chimney pipe on top, or through the open door, depending on the sophistication of the operation. Clear, bland, watery liquid that bubbles in the evaporating pans, soon becomes a sweet amber coating for pancakes and waffles. But sap won't run without the right conditions.

I lived in Vermont for a year and a half as a young teenager. Locals made sugar on snow for a party treat, or even dessert for supper. Their family tapped maple trees for the sweet, sticky sap. They boiled the sap to 235 degrees F., well beyond the temperature of 218 degrees for maple syrup, and transformed it into a taffy-like substance. We spooned ribbons of the thick, hot liquid over a dish of fresh packed snow. Instantly, the sugary syrup became a twirl-able mass chilled by the snow. If you started it with your fork, you could wind it like spaghetti and pop it in your mouth. The first time I tried it, my teeth got stuck in the hardening mass and clamped my jaws tightly shut. I had to wait for the maple candy to soften again before I could release my teeth. I learned to wind a small amount at a time around my fork, one strand of spaghetti instead of the whole plate in a giant ball.

The accompaniments–unglazed raised donuts and big crunchy spears of dill pickles, offset the intensely sweet taste of the reduced maple syrup. The combination brings grimaces to the faces of those who only hear the description of that union, instead of plunging into the bizarre flavor explosion. The bland fried dough balances the cloying sweetness, and biting into a sour pickle returns the pallet to neutral.

Maple taffy, doughnuts, and dill pickles sounded like a strange combination, but when I tried it, I found it burst with flavor and filled me with delight. Life must be experienced to be enjoyed, like writing, traveling, or any other adventure. To appreciate its challenges and rewards, it cannot simply be described.

My Lopsided Life

The pictures in my sunroom hang askew; no matter how many times I straighten them they return to their lopsided stance. In one, a seagull soars into the indigo opening within a puffy cloud. He flies through me, grabbing my spirits in his beak and carrying them up, shaking the dust and cobwebs from my mind and says, "Find your own way, overcome obstacles, and fly." The picture's square silver rim never stays level for more than a few seconds. Like my mind, I tidy and put things in order, but when I'm not looking, everything slides off balance and I must begin again.

On the seagull's right hovers a garden of purple, pink, and mauve flowers growing beside the sea. A peaceful spot, and when my gaze lands there my mind slows, the chatter quiets. It remains level longer, but eventually it too will revert to its crooked stance.

The last picture to the left of center contains a photograph of the view from my garden window of the snowy yard. A pot of paper whites provides the focal point. They appear to grow despite the snow, oblivious to the cold, but if you look closely, you can see they actually live inside a warm sunroom. Like many things in life, this one takes more effort to set aright, because it isn't the exterior, but the photograph inside that slides out of place.

Occasionally, I right the frames as I walk by. A few days later, I study each in turn and find them tilted once more. They represent the balancing act of my life—high above the circus tent, walking the tightrope of being and feeling, and searching for the perfect spot of steadiness and comfort. I can find no way to stay there and move forward at the same time. A gust of wind catches me and I almost fall, flailing my arms to steady myself. So much to do, so many things seeking a place in my life—my family, my friends, my garden, my writing, and me.

I want to spend time with family and friends. I miss them when I don't see them, but sometimes I miss me. Am I selfish to want space around me? Guilt wraps around me when I think I'm neglecting my friends, when someone wants me to do something and I can't, and I don't want to shut them out. I attempt to restore order, make a plan, have a schedule and follow it. I try to accomplish all the things on my to-do list; then the vibrations of life, like footsteps past my pictures, send everything off balance again. Some things stay level longer, they hold fast to their ordered state, but others go awry almost as soon as I reach out a steadying hand.

Life moves on. I can't see where to take the next step. Will I be able to make it across the wire and stay balanced? I am overflowing, then I am empty. How do I keep myself comfortably full? In my imagination, I set aside time to write every day and never waiver. I am productive in my constancy. I also visit my distant family, keep my house clean, sort drawers and closets, mow the lawn, work in the garden, exercise regularly, and take food to ailing friends—without fail. Reality paints a less perfect picture. The hours and days evaporate long before I finish my list. I want to read and have time to think, time to feed my soul.

What do I relinquish in order to keep the painting of my life level? How do I prevent it from becoming instant-ly skewed? I don't know, but I start by giving thanks for all of my life, including its lopsided parts.

Home

$\mathcal{I}$ live in a big house for one person. Some days I think I should sell it and move to a smaller one. Then, I enter my sunroom; it has windows that face east, south and west. It fills with light early in the morning, and stays bright until dusk. I watch the sun make its gradual climb over the trees. In winter I can view the full ascent, but in spring and summer the leaves shadow the rise, dappling the light until it explodes in a yellow flash high above the ground. In winter, its warmth wriggles in and snuggles around a cold afternoon. It is my favorite spot in the house.

I sit in my writing chair, which glides if I choose, and write, read, or think. I sip my morning coffee before first light and say good morning to the world. I drink my afternoon tea in the lingering glow that ends the day. My labor sighs from the walls, along with the hours I spent applying primer and paint to brighten the dark paneling. The addition of a garden window connects the room to the outdoors, houses my indoor plants in winter and vegetable seedlings in spring. In the midst of a snowstorm, it provides a comforting place to sit and brightens the darkest winter day.

The screened porch that floats high above the backyard

offers the perfect place in summer to wake to the concert of songbirds declaring the day's arrival, or to sit at night and listen to nature's vespers. A lazy afternoon on the porch swing with a book gives respite from the heat and gardening chores. My upstairs bathroom satisfies my childhood dream of purple walls, a clawfoot tub, and the scent of lavender that fills the room.

I look forward to opening my front door in late June to see my climbing Blaze rose that nearly obliterates the arbor with clusters of bright, cherry-red blooms. The arbor marks the entrance to a chaotic cottage garden that reflects over forty years of tender care. Days of planting, weeding, watering, and pruning, and my senses are filled with enchanting fragrances, a vibrant color palette that changes with the seasons, and the buzz of bees and hummingbirds.

All these things help keep me here, but even more, the memories that live here and comfort me when I am sad or lonely hold me in place. The sounds of children's lively games emanate from the sunroom. I see three boys playing catch when it's too dark to do it outside, or being lost in intricate Lego buildings. Years of Christmas mornings, Thanksgiving dinners, birthday celebrations, nights of homework, proms, and new baby cries dwell within these walls.

Special mornings with my grandchildren live here too. As parents, the early hours that our babies keep wear us out. But I am an early riser by nature, so when my sons visited with their children, I responded to the first murmurs from the crib. I carried my grandchildren downstairs, fixed breakfast, and had some cuddle time to begin the day. I inhaled their sweet sleepy smells as we snuggled close under a blanket or with their warm, fuzzy pajamas. I rocked them and gave them the first bottle of the day. Sometimes we sat and watched the birds as they breakfasted at the feeders, and when they got older we played games.

I have enough bedrooms for my children and their families to visit and sleep here again; their presence fills the rooms, and I feel them tucked safely inside. They breathe their life into the space and it fills me with love and peace. How can I leave?

Open the Door

Open the door and take my hand,
The house where I live doesn't claim to be grand.
The walls, though sturdy, feel drafty too,
Can you hear the stories they tell to you?
Two mothers lived in the same small space,
The older one left with the gift of grace.
The younger one stayed and her family grew,
Their laughter echoed through time that flew.
What do you see in the rooms upstairs?
Both joys and struggles hide in there.
A mother's footsteps soft and sure,
Carries a child in arms secure.
The banister shines with sliding boys,
One after the other and filled with noise.
A family gathers with stories shared,
Cookies baked, and arms that cared,
Memories linger in every room
The piano echoes a familiar tune.
Winter days of cold and storm,
Nights of quiet by a fire warm.
Bedtime stories every night,
A tree that sparkled with bubbling light.

Lullabies sung in the rocking chair,
I hear them now, but no one's there.
Gentle hand on a fevered brow,
Supper's ready, come home now.
Homework done at a tiny desk,
A cat that sprawled and purred the best.
Days of friends and times alone,
Growing up in this old home.
Soccer balls hit the metal grate.
Lego towers hold the lonely weight.
Three little boys who soon became men,
Moved far away but return again.
These walls know pain but promise too,
I remember the hours I talked to you.
Pictures that cover the kitchen door
Hold treasured moments, and love even more.

Daffodils in the Woods

Out my sunroom window two daffodil blossoms wave from a small clump of green on the path into the woods behind my house. I wonder how they got there. I usually plant daffodils in the fall, deep in loosened garden soil. They sleep through the winter, then push through the dark earth until they find daylight and open their yellow blossoms on a warm spring day. But I didn't plant these flowers in any garden bed.

Today looms as another gray March day, cold and damp, with a rawness that homes in on your bones, typical of New England weather in early spring. Winter has not yet handed off the baton to Spring, and though Spring reaches for it, Winter holds tight, not quite ready to let go. In the fall, I drag leaves on a big plastic tarp from my lawn into the woods across this path, as it offers the single access through the stone wall that surrounds my yard. Still, in the midst of moldering leaves and discarded branches, on a path traveled by numerous feet, and a brown landscape absent of any other green life, this clump of yellow cheerfully blooms.

I'm tempted to pick the blossoms and bring them into the house. After all, they remain unapparent to passersby, unlike my front yard, that causes people to pause and enjoy the yellow wave that grows more abundant every day. No one sees these two daffodils, no one but me. Do I want to enjoy them inside, where I can press my nose into their petals and inhale their delicate sweet scent? Or do I want to contemplate this splash of color in the midst of the lifeless surroundings, reminding me that in the middle of the pandemic, I found splashes of joy—video calls with my grandson twelve hundred miles away. We drew pictures, and then shared them on the camera. Splashes of kindness—one neighbor left her phone number on my doorstep in case I needed anything, another brought a plate filled with Thanksgiving dinner, when I couldn't travel to be with my family for the holiday. "Goodness and mercy will follow me all the days of my life." I leave the daffodils in the woods, a reminder that in the midst of difficult times, I am blessed with splashes of joy and kindness, and I give thanks.

Holly Cakes

Some people find it easy to downsize, discarding things willy-nilly, but I don't. I have always loved to cook, and I enjoy trying new recipes. I often clipped them from newspapers and magazines, and my bookshelves overflow with cookbooks and folders of loose recipes, including my plastic recipe box. Large, colorful cardboard dividers separate each category, and some spill into the neighboring section.

I don't bake as much as I used to, and when I decided to reduce my recipe collection, I found it easy to discard a recipe cut from a magazine, or off a box of baking chocolate. However, the handwritten recipe cards or random slips of paper didn't feel the same. Time stretched on as I thought back not only to the circumstances when I received the recipe, but to the person who gave it to me. Many of my strongest memories lived in that box.

Holly Cakes, actually a delicious brown sugar bar cookie, came from my mother's friend, Lois Stone. When my father's job meant a relocation to Burlington, Vermont, a longtime friend connected my mother with his sister who lived there. On their house-hunting trip, my parents met Lois and her husband, Herb. The four became immediate friends. Herb and Lois invited my dad to have dinner with them many nights when he relocated ahead of us. On moving day, we arrived in Burlington late in the afternoon, but the moving van wouldn't come until the next morning. The Stones not only fed us dinner, but also provided beds for all of us for the night. Lois made dinner a festive event, with roast beef, mashed potatoes, and for dessert—Holly Cakes.

Other recipes also stopped my sorting process, as I fell into the well of memories too dear to be discarded. Cambridge Coffee Carnival, a dessert recipe from my friend Rosie, whom I've known for over forty years, reminded me of the week I spent with her at her Block Island summer home. We rode our bikes, swam, and made fresh blackberry pie. When we returned, she joined my boys and me for supper one night. We all loved the unusual dessert she brought, made with coffee, tapioca, and cream. Cambridge Coffee Carnival became one of our favorites.

I found it most difficult to discard the cards handwritten by my mother. We were alike in many ways; even my handwriting resembled hers. She also loved to bake and try new recipes, and we would swap them back and forth. We seldom made them as written but insisted on adding our own twist. My mother would bake for several days before a local bake sale. She often contributed as many as twenty different items. I found charts that she had devised, listing all the cakes, cookies, and breads she planned to make down one side, and every ingredient needed across the top. As I studied the handwritten recipe card for Boston Baked Bread, a bake sale favorite, I wondered, did she write it, or did I? I'm not sure, but I tucked it back in the box, safely wrapped in delicious memories.

The Memory Keeper

My memories live in a wooden box,
Tucked between grayed cards
Long flecked with stains of lard
And crumbs of sticky Snickerdoodles.
They wait in silence,
Nestled in the corner, packed in tight
Until I lift the lid and free them to take flight.
They wander through the cupboards of my mind,
Faded words precisely written,
Some dimmed beyond recognition,
Others holding hands with yesterday
Drawing faces in the air, as they float across the kitchen.
A hologram sits in the waiting chair,
Wrinkled hands reach out to guide
The tiny ones that hold a rolling pin,
And I tell her where I've been.

Cookies marked with raisins to form a monkey's face,
The kitchen door bursts open
Spilling cold and children into stove-warmed space.
Gentle voices whisper as I hold the wooden box
Vibrating with stories my ears alone can hear,
Though not clearly seen they shimmer for me there.
Memories cling together in one delicious spot,
I close the lid to keep them safe.
Discard them? I cannot.

Spring Bliss

I wait with anticipation for signs of spring—cool days lose their brittle crunch and the air floats in moist clouds as it settles around my shoulders on my morning walk. If I pay attention, it crawls into view like time-lapse photography—appearing first as a watercolor wash of palest chartreuse on the trees, and turning darker green every day. If I don't pay attention, it arrives in a sudden explosion—leaves blocking the sun, and the lawn in need of mowing overnight. On the first warm day, I breathe the softer air, the smell of the ground as it wakes and stretches, releasing its unique spring aroma of damp earth and life, and if I listen, I can hear the season change in the birds' morning songs.

As I walk this afternoon, I hear the spring peepers for the first time this year. The bass-croaking frogs, who inhabit not only this roadside swamp, but also the pond behind my house, counterbalance their high-pitched peeping. The frogs serenaded me the past few days as I worked in the yard and ate lunch with the windows wide open. The Swamp Side Chorus has declared an end to winter. Spring has arrived.

It wakes the bits and pieces that have been buried and sleeping through winter. After my walk, I stroll around

the circle of my front yard. Crocuses have exploded overnight. Where the first warm day found a few scattered
flecks of yellow, purple, and white, now clumps of color
speckle the bare, brown earth. Grass, if grown, would
hide their tiny stature, but the freshening earth provides
a background for them to paint. My insides smile at the
crocuses, and I tell them how beautiful they are. They look
happy, like someone randomly spatter-painted my yard.
The dark purple flowers hid within clumps of green yesterday, but today their velvety petals emerge as the border
to the painting.

The April day makes me beam. To me, April looks
pink, though I can't tell you why. Purple and yellow flowers bloom this time of year, and even the early Emperor
tulips provide brilliant red companions for the daffodils.
Pink tulips won't arrive until May, another pink month,
though the sun shimmers through May, making it transparent pink. April is solid, opaque pink.

I feel a skip of joy as I gather the tools of the day: clip-
pers, scissors, and trowel, along with the big, blue plastic
tarp, and my rake with the foam padded handle. Winter lingered past her welcome and left her mark behind.
Frost-bitten leaves guard the daffodil buds, but I leave
them untouched. I rake all the dried, rusty leaves that
have been keeping the garden warm, and trim the over-
grown thyme that would like to rule the world. I dig my
fingers into the ground, inhale its moist, springtime smell,
and make sure the iris feet have not been engulfed by the
shifting soil or winter sand. I prune the butterfly bush and
envision the huge purple blooms that will draw the yellow
swallowtail butterfly in the summer sun. A Cardinal calls

from a nearby tree, and so does a Phoebe, looking for their mates to discuss the perfect nesting spot they've found. I chat with them now and then, whistling to the Cardinal and "phoebeing" into the stillness.

My hands don't require thought or instruction in this quiet work; they move through the familiar tasks on their own. They leave my mind free to wander, but it doesn't. On a rainy or snowy day, I find my bliss in writing, and my mind scurries about, gathering words like acorns. Today I discover bliss in the garden, I enjoy the swinging cadence of my body at work, and my mind rests.

The Rocking Chair

𝒜 recent power surge, following a storm-induced outage, triggered a fire in my house. Smoke damage required repainting the living room walls and refinishing the floors. This morning, I write in a different chair in a different room than usual. The living room furniture blocks my writing chair on the sunporch. The rocking chair in my bedroom offers the only place to sit, except at the kitchen table.

The sun has not yet rounded the corner from east to south to shine on my notebook. Through the open window, I hear a finch, singing its heart out and waking the world with his trills. In the distance I can hear several more birds, including a Phoebe, maybe the one that woke me at 4:30 in the morning. Except for the birds, the world outside my window remains still, as early mornings do. The school bus has yet to arrive, and most people have not left for work, so no cars drive by.

I sit in my grandmother's old rocking chair that now lives in my bedroom. I can still see her sitting in it and braiding the colorful rugs she made every winter. My parents had the chair refinished for me before I gave birth to my first son over fifty years ago. I treasure it, though I sit here less often since I no longer have any babies. I rocked all three of mine every night before I put them down to sleep or when they cried in the night, and I unfailingly sensed my grandmother's soothing company.

As a child, if I felt ill or sad, my grandmother would take me on her lap and rock me, or sometimes I rocked myself if she was busy. Even when I rocked alone, I felt like I absorbed her comforting presence from the chair, as if her essence had soaked into the wood and it wrapped around me, healing my physical or emotional pain.

The chair's wooden arms store countless peaceful hours, and I want to draw in that peace and comfort now. I face two weeks of chaos. I have to weave around the furniture, including a piano in my kitchen, in order to shower, do laundry, or cook. I will no doubt spend many hours in the coming weeks in this familiar chair. For now, I am grateful that the fire didn't cause more serious damage. I will sit in her chair and immerse myself in my grandmother's strong will and soft heart, and let it steep me in her love.

Daffodil Daze

If you come to my garden in April, an explosion of yellow daffodils will greet you.

Daffodils have been my favorite flower since I was a child, and they exist in a category by themselves, the pinnacle of my flower choice. They provide a lesson in faith and hope. I plant bulbs in September and ignore them through the winter. Then they channel the warmth of the spring sun into those papery bulbs and explode it back from the earth into a carpet of yellow. They trumpet the sounds of spring to me, as clearly as any brass band. And yes, if you take the time to come close, they offer a slightly sweet scent that floats on the spring warmth.

I don't know why I love daffodils so much, maybe because when I was a child, they bloomed before any other flower in our garden. Maybe because they often bloom for my birthday in April—Mother Nature's gift to me. Maybe because they are the extroverts in the garden and balance my introverted tendencies. Maybe because of their tenacious spirit they will bloom despite the unexpected hardships of snow and cold. They bounce back from beneath the blanket of white that weighed them down, and still turn their heads toward spring. They exude cheerfulness. My garden flows into an ocean of yellow in April; waves of different varieties parade across my front lawn, greeting everyone who drives by with their cheery presence.

My favorite flower changes with the season. I like columbine in the spring, because they dance like colorful ballerinas over the garden; Oriental lilies in summer, when their intense fragrance permeates the garden; and chrysanthemums in the fall, because their pink blossoms linger through October, until the arrival of a killing frost. Still, I love daffodils the most.

When I come home, they form the welcoming committee, and I see a flood of yellow as I round the corner. I have planted over a dozen varieties of assorted sizes and colors, including the friendly, miniature Tête-à-têtes that bloom as soon as the buds break the ground, the all-white Mount Hoods, and the magnificent yellow King Alfreds. An added bonus—the marauding deer ignore daffodils, and the bulbs live for many years. I have thriving clusters that my parents planted over fifty years ago. They don't mind being relocated from one spot to another where they will happily multiply.

After the gray days of March, when the bitter wind slices through the heaviest jacket, their vibrant yellow bursts from the brown earth and proclaims the welcome end of winter. When I stand in the midst of the white Narcissus, the delicate, haunting fragrance floats on the breeze—the smell of spring. But unlike their beauty, that they generously share with the casual passerby, their aroma is a subtle gift, given only to those who take the time to stop, linger, and enjoy.

What Do I Value Most?

What do you consider your most valuable posses-
sion? Artwork, jewelry, or something else? I think
about this as I wander room to room, searching out secluded corners in closets and scanning the walls. I don't
own things that cost a large sum of money—no huge
diamond ring, no priceless art treasure. I have a basic TV
(my grandchildren say, "It's tiny"), and I don't even own
a dishwasher. Old figurines and knickknacks sit tucked
away in cupboards, but I doubt any of them carry any
great monetary value.

I see the picture of my grandparents on the mantle.
A framed photograph of each of my parents and one of
them together grace the piano. Another snapshot of my
parents on a visit to Prudence Island sits beside my favorite one of my Aunt Dotty, taken the last time I saw
her. I survey the pictures of my grandchildren as infants
and toddlers, and I feel their pudgy embrace. I hear them
calling me Nanny or Nanna. I remember my own boys
as children, and I study the picture taken when Eric and
Peter were in elementary school, and Adam had yet to
celebrate his first birthday. Now I know the answer. What
do I value most? Memories of time spent with my family—I am a memory keeper.

The pictures of my children mark the march of time: high school and college graduations, weddings, the arrival of their first child. The memories warm and pierce my heart. I breathe in their little boy smells as I gaze at their photo. They have become men now, with children of their own. I repeatedly return to the pictures of me holding each of my grandchildren as infants, sleeping in my arms or peeking over my shoulder, completely at peace and trusting me to keep them safe.

I gaze around my sunroom and sit amidst my indoor plants. I love gardening both inside and out, and I cherish my plants for the peace they bring me. But I treasure memories the most, in words, pictures, and in my mind. Time has winged feet and refuses to stand still for anyone or anything. I want to slow its progress, see my grandchildren more, travel more, enjoy my garden more, but time turns a blind eye to my desires and moves faster and faster. Memories soothe the rough edges of loss and pain and magnify the moments of joy that passing time leaves in its wake.

Laila

S ome people come into our lives for a few minutes, and yet the impact they have on us lingers for years. My friend and I were on our way to a baseball game in Boston. He said, "It's just a couple of blocks and we get on the T, then get off at Fenway Park." He decided it might be a little more complicated than that, because when we passed a woman leaning on a fence, he said, "Let's ask her for directions."

She looked up from her cell phone and smiled when we approached. "Are we going the right way to the T?" he asked.

She nodded, and speaking with an accent said, "I go that way too, I show you." She offered her assistance without hesitation, put her phone in her pocket, picked up her backpack, and slipped it on. Grateful for her help, we walked together.

"My name is Laila," she said, and we introduced ourselves and told her we were going to the baseball game.

She responded immediately. "Is easy. I can help you, I'm going to Park Street too." Laila's appearance was unremarkable: gray sweatshirt, black pants, dark hair pulled into a ponytail, slightly protruding teeth, and no makeup. But when she smiled, her brown eyes sparkled and she radiated joy. It could be otherwise, I realized, as her story unfolded.

Because of her accent I asked, "Where are you from?"

"Colombia. Turn here, is shorter." Laila knew all the shortcuts, and our ten-block walk passed quickly as we chatted.

"How long have you been here?" I said.

"Three years, I escape domestic violence. My sister say I must come where is safe." She showed us a scar across her throat, from a cut inflicted by her husband. I shivered involuntarily when I imagined her pain and being in her position. "I have daughter and I'm on my way home now. I work as nanny at the house back there." She smiled when she spoke about the little boy.

"He's named Damian, is fifteen months old. I have much love in my heart for him." By the end of our brief journey, and after experiencing the kindness she showed to two strangers, I knew she had much love in her heart for everyone.

We reached the entrance to the subway and followed her down the steps. We needed two round-trip tickets since we would be returning late at night and wanted to already have our tickets. I hadn't been on a subway since I rode it as a child in New York City with my family. No longer could you hand cash to a person and receive a token in return. Now you needed a CharlieCard, and you added money to it whenever it ran out. We didn't have a CharlieCard, nor could we find directions for obtaining one. The machine for buying a ticket with a credit card refused to work and spit my friend's card back at us. We had planned to meet my son and his family at the game, and I wondered if we would get there before the game started, or at all. I thought of the song about Charlie on the MTA, and "Will he ever return?" began playing in my head.

"I have extra CharlieCard. I give you this." Laila held out the card, scanned it, and showed us how to add ten dollars, more than enough to get us to the game and back. My friend punched in his credit card number to activate the card. This time the credit card worked. Laila showed us how to swipe it twice to enter the gate and guided us to the Red Line. We rode the short distance to Park Square together. "You want Green Line," she said and walked with us there before she said goodbye and went to board the Blue Line.

We thanked her for her help and when she hugged us both, I again glimpsed the line across her throat, a reminder of her painful life in Colombia. She could have been bitter, frightened, hiding from the world. Instead, Laila chose to be generous and kind, a guardian angel who helped two strangers. I only saw her briefly, and yet in those few moments, she touched me with her thoughtfulness. Would I do the same for strangers? I hope so.

Beyond the Pond

*T*he tiny pond behind my house glows gold in the morning. It lies beyond the first stone wall that rims my lawn, but before the second one, deeper in the woods, that marks my property line. I sip my coffee and watch the sun rise outside my window. It has yet to crest the tree line, but already long fingers of light play across the surface of the water. At certain times during the year the trees and vines, grown thick with age, hide the pond in their shadowy arms, making it undetectable from the house. But now, in early spring, the trees stand bare. The vines have not sent out their sinewy tendrils, and I have a clear view to the miniature oasis in the woods. Called a vernal pool, it comes and goes with the seasons. They naturally occur in some places, but this one began with my father's dream.

When he retired in 1978, my dad envisioned a park behind the house and had this pond dug. He planned to clear the undergrowth, and the few tall trees he allowed to remain would provide shade for woodsy strolls. His vision included trails through the trees and a bench or two for relaxing or sharing a picnic lunch in the shade beside the pond. But none of that except the pond came to pass. He died on Palm Sunday in April 1979.

When my boys were growing up, they skated there with little worry of falling through the ice. Because of its shallow depth, it froze solid before the larger local ponds. They constantly explored the surrounding woods, and their feet stamped out easily followed trails. Wild elderberry bushes grew in the sunny spots, and in fall the aroma of ripening Concord grapes floated over the backyard. I made jelly from both fruits for their lunchtime peanut butter and jelly sandwiches. The trees have grown and shaded the elderberries, or the deer have eaten them, and they have disappeared. Right now I can see into the woods, but soon that will be impossible; there are no little boy feet to keep the paths open. I seldom walk there in the summer, because I worry about ticks and Lyme disease, a new concern since my boys were children.

Occasionally, ducks glide across the water in their graceful landing pattern, grateful I think, for this sheltered rest stop on their journey north or south. I ask them to stay longer, or at least return often, but the space is too small, their visit a fleeting gift. I have seen an owl perched on a low branch in late afternoon, waking from his day of sleep, preparing for a night of hunting. A family of Red-tailed Hawks resides close by, and I see one perched near the pond. I hope he hunts for mice and doesn't search for songbird nests.

When the temperature warms in March or April, the frogs that call the pond home start croaking. A strange and wonderful sound, full of life and new birth, the raucous noise makes me smile, because it signals spring's arrival. I hear it before the skunk cabbage appears, and often before the first fat robin searches for worms in my front yard. The frogs wake when the ice melts, the mud thaws, and the pond fills with spring rain.

One hot August day I heard splashing in the woods. Normally the pond dried to a muddy hollow in August, but this had been a summer of endless rain. In the distance I saw two fawns chasing each other though the water. They leaped and ran in and out of the pond like two toddlers who had discovered a giant mud puddle. I expected to hear squeals of glee, but they resonated only in my mind. I saw the mother join her rambunctious children for a refreshing swim. She appeared to enjoy it as much as they did, and it reminded me of swimming at the local pond with my children.

When I started writing today, the pond shone like a smoldering ember in the woods. Now the sun has climbed higher. The tiny pool sits in darkness again, barely a glimmer below the blinding light aimed directly in my window. It glows across the page, highlighting my pen. The frogs have not yet awakened, and I wonder if I will hear them today. I listen to the call of a White-breasted Nuthatch as he courts his mate. I close my eyes and remember excited tales of explorations and building forts, when little boy feet still roamed through the woods, beyond the pond.

A Bittersweet Story

Sometimes I think I live in Sleeping Beauty's castle. Delete the image of a fanciful edifice adorned with imposing turrets and replace it with a white shingled farmhouse built in the mid-1800s. Sturdy and sound, with a warm, comforting presence I'm sure Sleeping Beauty's castle didn't possess. The resemblance to that magical castle is not in the building, but in the encroaching woods and vines that seem to creep closer and closer to the house every spring. Despite my efforts to control the bittersweet vines, they assert their homestead rights and continue to expand their piece of the territory. I long to see the beautiful stone walls surrounding my yard, but Mother Nature's evil twin has cast a spell on the vines. I swear I see them grow two feet for every foot I cut back, and the walls remain obscured.

Fifty years ago, homeowners considered bittersweet, which yields bright orange and yellow berries in the fall, a decorative vine. They made wreaths for their doors, added them to floral arrangements, and allowed them to climb over walls and fences. When my parents bought this house, they planted bittersweet on the property. In recent years, gardeners have realized that the colorful plant is invasive. The vines will usurp anything in its path unless you are relentless in their demise. They will claim the trees, the house, the yard, the drainpipes, even the wheelbarrow if it sits idle for too many days.

Bittersweet travels underground, creating a network of orange wires, and reappears far from its original source. I once freed a cluster of daffodils from the clutches of a gnarled bittersweet root several inches in diameter. Once out of the ground, it resembled a large piece of driftwood, so I painted it purple and used it as a lawn ornament.

Occasionally, spring weather interferes with reclaiming the castle and its surrounding stone walls from the clutches of the bittersweet. A few years ago, several feet of snow, also known as poor man's fertilizer, fell during the winter and still covered the ground in early April. The invading vines grew as if given steroids. Grapevines extended over the stone walls and crept into the yard, while the bittersweet encased the poles that support my screened porch, climbed the gutters, and wove in and out of the woodpile. I knew it would assail the windows next, creeping through the cracks and preventing them from shutting, or find its way under the shingles, lifting them off the house and flinging them to the ground.

An early spring means I can get a head start on the ravaging vines; of course it also means the bittersweet obtains a head start too. Like Sleeping Beauty, I need a Prince Charming to rescue me. However, I do not require a kiss to end a seven-year sleep, but strong arms and a stout heart to defeat the evil bittersweet.

May 24

In this moment, I sit down to write, and my phone pings with a notice of pictures of my new grandson, Desi. In this moment, I am grateful for his safe arrival ten days ago. In this moment, I want to reach into the phone and hold him close, sing him a song, and smell his new baby scent. In this moment, I want him to know how much his Nana loves him, even if we've never met. In this moment, my heart fills, and spills over with tears from my eyes. He lives so far away. It will be weeks before I can see him. In this moment, I focus on the love that surrounds him, how much Oliver likes being a big brother, and seeing him in *my* baby's arms, their proportions so extreme—Adam's hands the size of Desi's body.

In this moment, I start my day with coffee and prayer, pen and paper, as I wake with the world. In this moment, the sun wraps its arms around me, replacing the early morning chill with its warmth, and glistens on my notebook. In this moment, I start writing with a smile on my face and enjoy what is. In this moment, the world stays quiet, slow to rouse on a Saturday morning, no traffic, no lawnmowers or leaf blowers, just an insistent bird chirping his excitement in the day.

The pink Josie lilac has exploded, and scented, deep

purple clusters envelop the lilac beside my front door. In this moment, a list of things to do sits somewhere, longer than I want to see, calling to me, but in this moment, I am filled with elation for this new baby. In this moment, the weeds can wait. I'll walk soon, but in this moment, I will look at you, as you yawn, and stretch, and find your fingers. In this moment, you patiently wait, trusting you will soon be fed. In this moment, I'll be patient too, waiting to hold you. In this moment, I will savor where I am, my coffee cup beside me, the garden waiting to fill me with its fragrance. I'll set your photos aside and enjoy life here, in this moment, knowing I'll meet you soon. The compost will be spread, the window boxes planted, the birthday cake for Owen made, more words written, but in this moment, knowing you are here in this world, and loved, is enough.

Ferry Ride

When the alarm goes off at 6:30, I am still sound asleep, and I wake to a chilly, gray day. Normally, I would shut off the alarm and tuck myself under the covers for another nap. But not today. Today I'm going to Prudence Island, and I don't have to force myself out of bed. Excitement propels my body from sleep as I prepare for my first trip this season and anticipate falling under the island's spell again. Does everyone who rides the ferry feel this way? I don't know, but I know I feel like I've been given ice cream, cake, and a ride on the merry-go-round all on the same day.

Incessant traffic crawls through Providence at five or ten miles an hour, and my anxiety builds. The ferry won't wait. By the time I get to Bristol, I long for a strong cup of coffee, but I can't find a parking place in the usual lot. *Now what?* I think. I find a temporary space, buy my ticket, and obtain a pass which allows me to park on the street for the day. I search for a spot, and a Prudence guardian angel watches over me. A red pickup truck pulls out, and I drive into the vacant place right beside the walkway to the ferry landing. I breathe a relieved sigh and the tension gripping my shoulders eases. I have time to walk the few blocks to my favorite bagel shop, Bristol Bagels. I fortify myself with coffee and a fragrant, warm cranberry-walnut bagel, chewy on the outside, tender and moist in the middle.

I return to the car and don my backpack. Although it's a day trip, I carry everything I might want while I'm on the island: my writing tools, a book, my lunch, and extra clothes. The island can be bone chilling on a damp day. One hand loops through the handles of the green shopping bag that carries tomato and coreopsis plants for my friend Judy, and I hold my coffee cup in the other. I lock the car and board the ferry with five minutes to spare.

Across the bay, Poppasquash Point floats in a sea of gray. Prudence grows larger on the horizon. When I step off the ferry, I forget the trials of the morning. I feel the island's gentle squeeze. It lingers as a hug should: not a fleeting touch, but a full body embrace that envelops every part of me. My euphoria takes off across the beach, down dirt roads, and over open grass where clothes dance on the lines. I return the embrace, drawing close to breezes gusting off the water, turtles peeking from the pond searching for sun, hummingbirds flitting beneath the porch roof, and quiet.

The silence whispers of the absent sounds of the world, no horns honking, no engines revving, no radios blaring. I hear the stillness. I hear the waves tumbling on the beach, playing with the rocks, and the call of distant gulls. I hear the songbird symphony, with solo trills and ensembles. The glider creaks, and I breathe in the island.

I am part of it, and it soaks into the sinew of my being and lifts my spirits. My heart surges with gratitude to be in this place that nourishes my mind and body and brings sunshine to my soul.

Prelude to Write

Captiva and Prudence Islands exist worlds apart. One basks in tropical breezes and bathes in warm Gulf waters, the other swims in chilly Narragansett Bay, buffeted by cold northeast winter winds. Anne Morrow Lindbergh wrote *Gift from the Sea* on Captiva Island in Florida. The beaches she walked and the surf she heard belonged to Captiva, but the salt air and wave songs her words elicit in me, live in my Prudence Island soul.

A friend gave this book to me when I was in the midst of raising children, working, returning to school for my teaching certification, and teetering on the brink of divorce. On a day when I thought I would lose my grip on sanity, I picked it up and started to read. It didn't solve any problems, it didn't even make them less severe, but it did spawn a tiny island of peace in the tsunami of my life, a place where I could breathe, say ahhh and move on.

Lindbergh wrote *Gift from the Sea* in 1955. She was on her own quest for peace and balance in her tumultuous and busy life. She wondered how to simplify the demands everyday life created and find her place in the world. Although our lives were vastly different, I searched for many of the same things she did, and I returned to this book again and again every time my life felt unbalanced; I would read it and I would breathe.

She searched for a way to carry lessons from the sea home with her. A peace Lindbergh said is born of simplicity, solitude, and intermittency. I feel this way every time I visit Prudence. I want to pocket the island's peace and carry it back to Chepachet.

Island life teaches simplicity. When Lindbergh spoke of her island vacation home, I pictured summer houses on Prudence Island. The trappings of life are unnecessary; we eat outside on the porch and outdoor showers suffice. I live on island time, without deadlines or to-do lists. I have space in the day to listen to the birds or take a walk, visit with friends, or sit and read. I have time to be, and a bathing suit and a towel are all I need. Why can't I be happy without so much stuff in Chepachet? If I don't need it on Prudence, why do I need it at all?

Island life teaches solitude. We all need solitude. Sometimes it comes in drops, sometimes in buckets. A drop often doesn't seem enough. I used to hold on to my drops of solitude and cherish them. I lived in a house with three boys, and when I felt desperate for breathing space, where I knew they wouldn't follow me, I would take a bath. For a few minutes I would sink into a tub of scented water and breathe, ahhh. Now I have buckets of solitude, and sometimes I think I will drown in them.

When my youngest son went off to college, I came home every day after teaching high school, to an empty house. My baths could be as long as I wanted, I had no one to escape from except myself. I had to relearn to be comfortable with solitude, at peace with my own company. I had to remember the lesson of solitude I learned from Prudence. On my worst days, I reread *Gift from the Sea,* and my soul breathed, ahhh. I'm not alone in my solitude. Isn't that what we all long for? To know we are not the only one to feel this way?

Life and love both have an ebb and flow, one tide does not negate the one that preceded it, one is not better than the other, just different. When one stage of life morphs into the next, it doesn't mean the previous stage wasn't meaningful. The tide ebbs and flows twice every day, and the Horseshoe, my favorite swimming spot on Prudence, fills completely. Then twice a day the slippery rocks and stony shore emerge. Each has its own gifts, its own rewards. When the tide ebbs, creating a wide expanse of rocky shore, I search out the sweet clams that hide submerged in the mud. I dig with my fingers, mindless of broken nails or my hard stone chair. I absorb the sun's warmth on my back and the bay's quiet in my mind. Swimming presents a struggle now, requiring a walk over slippery rocks and exposed barnacles, but the ebb tide rewards me with fat clams that I lift from the mud. Gradually the tide flows in, filling the Horseshoe, covering the clams and the slippery rocks with the sea. Now I can float off the ladder into the cool bay without touching the bottom.

Relationships ebb and flow like the sea. Even the best relationships have challenges. That thought has stayed with me through relationship highs and lows and through the pain of loss. When in the midst of a difficult time, I reached for this book and reminded myself of life's ebb and flow. I read and the storm calmed, if only on my small island of words, and I could breathe again, ahhh.

The first time I went to a writing class, my life felt out of balance. I was searching for something, but I didn't know what, and I wrote about the peace I find on Prudence Island. At the end of the class the group leader said, "Have you ever read Anne Morrow Lindbergh's *Gift from the Sea?*" Ahhh, I will write, and breathe.

Summer

Island Summer House

Salt-grayed shingles sit high above the sand-less shore,
Scanning the changing tide as it fills the horseshoe cove.
Hidden slippery rocks draw young swimmers to their edge,
And clammers must have patience to scour supper from
    the mud.

Timeless August days meander in the sun,
One becomes another as morning trickles into noon.
Hypnotic blue and chintz soft chairs, eclipse the list
    of chores,
And supper waits for sunset to waft its smells across
    the lawn.

An evening chill arrives, fetching jackets from their hooks,
Sending diners within lamplit walls, sharing tales of
    summer gone.
Wooden arms reach out to hold them close before they flee,
Pleading, "One more story, one more night," soon
    they'll hurry on.

The lock key turns, the screen door slams one final time,
Quiet clutches the dwindling sound that follows the
    scattered dust.
Hungry gulls survey the barren porch for treats
    they left behind,
While memories of laughter echo within, ears stay
    pricked for their return.

Mindless ghosts of summer bask in the waning sun,
The creaking glider stands silent, hidden from the
    passing breeze.
Ragged sneakers, all soles and laces, languish on the
    clam hod slats,
Still more vestiges of summer are stashed behind a
    bunk bed screen.

Mournful eyes gaze across the bay, past the
    neighbor's silhouette,
Enduring the sea's unyielding charge, led by ice and snow.
Its moans and sighs reverberate under the punishing winds
As mice and cold creep in, its brittle bones ache for
    their return.

Relentless waves undulate towards shore, concealed by
    frozen foam,
And the cries of an orphan wind chime drift over the
    muffled surf.
Sightless eyes reflect the sunset's flame, orange glows
    on shingles gray,
Still standing lonely watch, waiting for their return.

The wind abates, its wails transformed to whispers,
Deep breaths instead of shuddering sighs, can be resumed.
Air, sun-warmed and dried, seeks every chill damp corner,
As empty chairs and old porch tables, prepare their
    welcome home.

Salt-grayed shingles stand listening, waiting for the news,
The sound of a distant motor as wheels grumble
    through rain-soft ruts.
The car springs squeak, the lock key turns, the screen
    door slams once more.
Footsteps pound and laughter bursts, they have returned.

My Memory Triggers

A Catbird chats from the tree beside me as I sit on the grass weeding. We converse amicably and he floats around from branch to branch watching me work and offering suggestions. I think he enjoys my company as much as I enjoy his. The sun warms my back but doesn't cook me. When I weed, my mind feels free. Sometimes it goes nowhere, like a Canary who prefers the safety of his cage to flight, even when someone leaves the door open. I don't need to think about what I'm doing, my hands and eyes recognize the weeds, my brain observes, but rests. My thoughts drift, a canoe not paddled, but aimlessly riding the gentle currents of my mind.

For a while, silence envelops the road by my house; my neighbors must be resting in the summer heat. The birds chat in whispers and provide a calming background buzz that lulls me across the bay to Prudence Island. I enter a time machine that transports me from my current life to my six-year-old life, and I find myself back in my childhood home when I had nothing pressing to do. The sun heated the soft air in my yard. A cat waited to be petted, a doll to be held, and a mudpie to be made, all in silence, except for the crickets, the birds, and the hum of summer.

Summer should be for idle days of reading and

swimming, sitting on the rocks and watching the water, bike rides, ice cream, and lazy love. Now I find myself sneaking time to read a book, and whenever I do, I feel like a recalcitrant child who slips out of the house to play, and hears her mother say, "Don't forget to do your chores before you go outside." I push quietly through the screen door when she isn't looking, and when the reprimand comes, "You were supposed to finish your chores before you went out to play," I don't argue or claim forgetfulness, that would be a lie. I didn't forget, I wanted to play. I respond with a noncommittal, "Oh," and don't say another word. I didn't feel guilty taking time for myself then, why do I now?

I love the process of spontaneous remembering. I wrote my first book this way, and I continue to bring into being an occasional poem or story in this manner too. I hear a specific sound, or sometimes I breathe myself through time and space. I go for a morning walk on a gray autumn day, and the aroma of burning leaves hangs in the still, misty air. I float on it, like a cartoon character, drifting, nose attached to a stream of smell, back to Prudence Island, to a fall evening when my bedtime came before dark, and I stood by my bedroom window watching my parents raking and burning leaves in the backyard below; or I meander back to my teenage years—football games and walking home from school, afternoon bike rides stretching as far as I could pedal and still be home before dark, while around me the sweet, dry scent of burning leaves wafted from the yards I passed.

I pull more weeds and absorb the summer silence. My mind often races frenetically around the house or yard, thinking of all I need to do, even when my body remains still. But not today—today my mind rocks gently on waves of peace and solitude. It swings back and forth on the glider of the day that soothes and allows me to relax, unhurried in the moment, here in this one spot.

We can ignore these memory triggers, become so engrossed in our activities and daily tasks, that we leave no room for wandering into the memory nooks and crannies in the mansion of our mind. We think our stories and memories don't matter, but they do; they tell us who we are, and if we don't stop and listen, it will be too late to share and preserve them.

Fog

The fog hangs low this morning, quieting the world and muffling the insects, a motionless curtain without a breeze to shimmer it. A persistent Cardinal pierces the gray, calling to his mate, and she answers, one chirping note repeated three times.

"Where are you?"

"I'm checking on the house. Do you want to go for coffee?"

"Yes, come here and we'll go together." He moves away, his voice growing fainter as he flies from the tree outside my window to her side, deep in the woods. When she calls once more, silence answers; he found her, and all is well. A car races by outside my open window. I write as I hear my neighbors leave for work. The school bus will soon rumble past, and the sun slithers through the gray; heat will stalk the day again. I'll walk before it becomes too hot to breathe, before the fog turns to suffocating steam and I am shower-drenched when I return, before it grows too hot to clean upstairs.

I stand in the doorway of the bedroom where my boys, Eric, Peter, and Adam, slept as children. When the older two moved, first to their own rooms, and then on to college, this room became Adam's alone. Now my grandchildren sleep here when they visit. This room speaks memories, breathes them into the air; they ride the dust motes and rippling curtains, climb the white walls lined with narrow stripes of red, yellow, and blue, sleep in the two twin beds where cribs once stood.

I browse through all the books, especially the ones I read over and over at bedtime: *Good Night Moon, Runaway Bunny, Leo the Late Bloomer,* and I feel a pain of loss in my heart and my soul. My children have grown, become responsible, caring men with families of their own, and I am grateful every day for that. But I miss their constant presence and hugs, their scent of outdoors and tousled hair, and their smiles and giggles.

I catch a fleeting glimpse of them in my grandchildren, but even they are growing older, two now teenagers, and three live too far away for frequent visits. Too far away to sleep in this room designed to hold a child's memories, to comfort his pain, and provide a canvas for her imagination. I sort and tidy the bookshelves, and discard torn and used coloring books. I will donate the books with no memories attached to the library, but I give myself permission to tuck the others, well-read and memory-filled, back on the shelf. I'm not ready to part with them quite yet.

Rhode Island Summer Generations

We pay our toll on the Mount Hope Bridge, summer
    has begun.
School vacation opens, with a day in the Newport sun.
We park our car in wispy grass, alongside Second Beach,
Then gaze across the soft white sand, as far as sight
    can reach.
We grab our towels from the car, and a jug of lemonade,
A cooler filled with sandwiches, the ones my mom has made.
Endless foam-topped swells roll in, upon the tidal rush,
We spread two blankets on the sand, and baby oil on us.
We top our curly hair with bright flowered bathing caps,
And squeal when any icy wave hits us with a smack.
Our bodies work as surfboards, we swim till time for lunch,
Then eat our tuna sandwiches, pickles add a crunch.
We rest for one whole hour, swim until we have to go,
Our faces now shine lobster red, and warm from the
    sun's glow.
We head home with one last stop, at Newport Creamery,
An ice cream cone to end our day, I choose strawberry.

Flash forward twenty-five years ahead,
We drive to Scarborough Beach instead.
Three boys, three girls, and two busy moms,
Head to the shore with much aplomb.
The oldest three line the wide back seat,
They hold three more, with dangling feet.
Pack towels, drinks, and a yummy lunch,
Bring along snacks for the kids to munch.
Since they have grown past baby stage,
We skip Sand Hill Cove, to find bigger waves.
First spread sunscreen with a generous hand,
Then dive into the surf or stretch on the sand.
The youngest two build fine castles tall,
Two moms sit and watch over them all.
They chat and laugh but don't look away,
Their eyes never leave their children at play.
As an orange sun slides into the sea,
We gather the blankets and shake the sand free.
On the way home, we all vote to stop,
Oatley's for ice cream will make our day tops.
I order Grape-Nut, a Rhode Island treat,
Return to the car, our excursion complete.
Two tired moms still ride home with big smiles,
Six sleepy children take naps all the while.

Flash forward once more, another thirty-five years,
When five grandchildren arrive with loud, joyful cheers.
They've packed towels, and shovels, and also their pails,
Brought one boogie board, across the shallows to sail.
Roger Wheeler State Beach earns our choice for safe play,
Now grandchildren's giggles swell my heart and the day.
They fill buckets with shells, to take home on the plane,
Add a collection of rocks, to paint if it rains.
When they tire of digging in the coarse, crusty sand,
We explore and find swings, but we keep holding hands.
I give each one a push, and make each one fly high,
Then they soar on the swings like the gulls in the sky.
Our trip ends with a taste that cannot be beat,
We stop by at Brickley's, for ice cream cones sweet.
It will always hold true, though so many years pass,
Summer days at the beach, create memories that last.

Friendship

S andy sat in the back of Mrs. Talbot's fifth-grade class
at Primrose Hill School, her blonde hair flipped at
the ends. I had recently moved from Prudence Island.
I had attended a one-room school on the island, where
my fourth-grade class had two students. When I walked
into my fifth-grade class on the first day of school, I was
suffused in culture shock, and I shrank beneath the stares
of twenty-five unfamiliar faces. Then Sandy smiled at me,
and her green eyes crinkled at the corners. She had an
established circle of friends, but she opened it and invited
me in, introducing me to her best friend, Meredith, and
then I had two new friends.

We lived about two miles apart; I lived on the main
road, she lived on a quiet back street, and I would ride
my bike there to play. I was overjoyed when my parents
bought the house next door to Sandy's the summer before
we entered tenth grade. Our backyards ran together, and
our friendship blossomed. We spent Friday afternoons in
her kitchen eating potato chips and drinking Coca-Cola,
or we would go to my house and play duets on the piano
while my grandmother cheered us on. For the first time,
my best friend lived next door.

Some friends sit on the surface, never melding into

the rich colors of our existence. Others paint themselves into our lives, their presence as necessary as our own to make the image come alive. They add depth, like good wine, rich in years and mellow in disposition.

Friendship sustains us, it provides a life vest that keeps us afloat when rough waters heave us from the boat. Sometimes we become the life ring tossed into the waves. Our friends hold on, and we pull them to shore. At times we must wade into the water and offer our hand, when life's burdens weigh so heavily they prevent a friend from swimming, even with a life vest. Another longtime friend laughed and cried with me through the years; she lifted my spirits when they sagged. Then *she* needed a life ring to pull her through troubles rough and battering to her soul. The calm waters of life had gradually become a raging ocean, hurling her into waves each bigger than the next. I wondered if I could hang on, if I could pull her to safety or if I would have to let go, and trust that the ship speeding towards her would arrive in time.

When friends become part of us, their loss feels like layers of our own skin being flayed one painful layer at a time. Friendship isn't just secrets shared over tea and cookies, or soothing a broken heart when a romance ends. It isn't just homemade soup delivered when you have the flu, or a Scrabble game while a blizzard rages outside. It isn't just a comforting presence to ease the overwhelming grief when a loved one dies, or company in the pain of lingering loneliness. It isn't just a walk to lift your spirits or sharing memories of the past with laughter and love. It isn't just adult conversation in the midst of children's endless needs and cries, or lunch on a depressing day. It isn't just daily prayer for the healing of mind, body, and soul, but it is all of these and more.

Friendship is a gift, a blessing in life, a view of God's love through another. Friendship acknowledges the faults but rejoices in the strengths, and it accepts us as we are, unclothed in the masks that we wear for the world. It sees the best shining through and nurtures the seeds of greatness hidden deep inside. Friends shape who we are. They blot the pain of loneliness and plant gardens of beauty and joy in our hearts.

Sandy's friendship was all of these, and it spanned sixty-five years of writing to boys and planning dates, riding bikes, and going to the beach. Sixty-five years of weddings, births, and loss, our parents, her husband and sister, my marriage.

As we both stepped into retirement, and she had to battle cancer for a second time, I tried to capture special moments on the page: our week together after her hip replacement, Christmas shopping in a newly discovered candy store where we found treasures for our grandchildren, but treasured more the fun we had together. We relied on a friendship that remained solid in joy and in sorrow.

I have been blessed with friendships like Sandy's that spanned decades. Constant, caring friends who left me diminished when they passed, and made me more because of their presence in my life.

The Lady in the Pink Turban

I donned my favorite lavender earrings, and Aunt Dotty's pink turban-capped face shimmered next to me in the mirror. In my mind, I heard her say, "Looking good, Toots."

Dorothy was my father's younger sister. She grew up in Brooklyn, New York, one of seven children and the older of the two girls. I have no recollection of meeting her as a child, although she told me she visited our family on Prudence Island as a teenager.

On a cross-country trip, my husband and I planned to stay with Aunt Dotty in California for a night or two. It quickly grew into a week-long visit. Aunt Dotty and I bonded like long-lost sisters. Despite our different backgrounds, we found a common thread of connection. We shared the same sense of humor, loved the same expensive perfume, and were enchanted by the same rides when we visited Disneyland. We both had a creative streak, although mine formed a brushstroke compared to her complete, detailed picture.

Like Mary Poppins, she flew in on the west wind one day, a carpetbag clutched in each hand, their weight causing her to waddle slightly when she walked. Unlike Mary Poppins' prim and proper attire, her loose slacks and tunic flowed and rustled around her. The summer breeze lifted golden brown curls from her smooth, unwrinkled face. Full coral lips smiled in delight and rings sparkled on her fingers. Her very presence was captivating.

Whenever Aunt Dotty visited, she always arrived bearing special gifts for my children and me. "I brought you a few things," she'd say as she opened one carpetbag. Like Mary Poppins, she withdrew an endless stream of treasures—small toys, books, and games for the boys and a blue sweatshirt with a sailboat heeling in the wind and "California" emblazoned across the top, for each of them. Magically, she brought the right sizes for everyone, including a pink one for me, with blue lettering over the sailboat that said, "Someone in California Loves You." After over thirty years of wear, I can see through it if I hold it to the light, but as long as it is in one piece, it stays.

"I thought you'd like these," she said, handing me an exquisite pair of earrings with lavender stones suspended from delicate silver wires. These were followed by a gold ring that cradled a pale pink stone, a silver filigree necklace with a square-cut amethyst nestled inside, and a small, round, woven hatbox to hold the jewelry. Her generosity touched me, as did her ability to know exactly what I would like.

"I painted this for you," she said, and withdrew a post-card-size picture of a lake, surrounded by mountains and pine trees, and framed in bright blue and gold. I fully expected to see a floor lamp emerge as well, but she had finally reached the bottom of the bag.

Dotty embraced life with pragmatism and joy. She could play the piano and accordion by ear, create precise miniature canvases, and her comedic sense of timing kept me in hysterics when she told stories about being the mother of twins. Sprinkled with whimsy, she held an innocent wonder about the world, despite spending most of her childhood in foster homes, which had not been safe for a beautiful young girl.

On her last trip east, she attended my oldest son's wedding. My favorite picture of her, taken at the wedding reception, showed her wearing a pink turban that matched her flowing pink pants suit, blowing bubbles through a tiny wand.

Through the years, Aunt Dotty recounted events from her difficult childhood and the feelings that accompanied them. She told me stories about my dad that he had never shared and opened a door of understanding that had been tightly shut my entire life. I began to appreciate my father, the man I had both loved and feared, and that was the true gift she gave me over thirty years ago, when she blew in on the west wind.

I walk...

The air this morning hangs thick with moisture, like moss draped on the trees in a Mississippi bayou. Although the sun still floats on the horizon, I already know my face wears a glistening sheen that reflects the light. The birds don't sing as exuberantly as they do on a crystal-clear morning, but still I walk—three or four miles every day, unless severe weather makes it unsafe.

As a child, I loved to walk or run and the need to move never left me. When I am filled with joy and think I might burst, I walk. As a high school senior, I applied for a $1000 scholarship for my freshman year in college, even though I had little hope of receiving it. When I learned it had been awarded to me, I couldn't believe it, nor could I sit still, so I walked a mile to the corner store and bought a kite. Although I never flew the kite, the idea of it captured the feeling I had inside me—of soaring high above what I anticipated.

When I have a decision to make or a puzzle to solve, I walk. As an adult with three children, I returned to school for my teaching degree. I had multiple papers to write and back then, I went for a run, organized my thoughts, and then came home and wrote. Today, I walk, and though I don't cover the ground quite as quickly, I achieve the same results—I sort my thoughts and come home with a plan. I wrote two books this way.

If I have argued with a friend or am faced with a difficult conversation, I walk. The issues stream through my mind from every angle. I hold silent discussions, consider alternate points of view, and diffuse my stress or anger. When I am grieving and I can't find a place to put myself, I walk. I allow the tears to wash my cheeks, and though my grief doesn't end, I feel better prepared to face it. When my mother died, my four-mile walks stretched to five or six, even after a day spent teaching. Each time I crest a hill, and there are many where I live, I feel a sense of accomplishment that keeps me going, and I know with time and more walks, I will heal.

I walk when I have cabin fever in the winter. It doesn't matter if the snow falls, I take to the back roads and I walk. The few cars that pass me go slowly, the engine noise muted by the falling snow. I don't solely travel along the back roads and undiscovered regions of the small town where I live, I also explore the cavernous reaches of my mind. I ruminate and discover unexpected gems, like the sea glass you find on the beach, smoothed to clarity by rolling over and over in my subconscious. If I find jagged edges, left by the memories themselves or because they haven't tumbled long enough, I set them aside to ponder on another day.

When I walk, I observe the world around me with new eyes, notice the changes in sounds, colors, and the air from season to season. The details I see matter, the moments I notice and remember matter, and so I walk.

Growing Anticipation

The catalog arrived by mail
Midst white and swirling snow,
Stirring thoughts of coming spring
And the tomatoes I would grow.

One of every thirty kinds,
Well, maybe make it three,
Enough to feed the neighbors,
The woodchucks, deer—and me.

Tiny seeds hold promises,
I water them and wait.
They sleep beneath the fertile soil,
Until with time, they wake.

Spindly arms reach towards the sky,
Hands clasping overhead.
Do you tire of standing tall
When you leave your cozy bed?

Round and sweet, black cherry red,
Hide in filaments of green,
Anticipation brings rewards,
Though they still remain unseen.

Now frost no longer threatens,
Fresh-mown grass scents the air,
With a trowel I dig deep holes
Then nestle plants safely there.

Today I reach the garden
Beneath the Blue Jay's din,
I bite into my sun-warmed snack,
And the Juice Runs Down My Chin!

BLT

I eat a BLT once a year, in the summer, when the native tomatoes arrive. Rhode Island has a short tomato season. The first varieties usually ripen in late July, or sometimes not until early August, and they disappear by the end of September. I don't eat bacon on a day-to-day basis; in fact I no longer eat pork or beef. Pork left fifteen years ago and I haven't eaten beef in twenty-five years. I could eat turkey bacon, but when I make a BLT, I want the real thing: bacon from a pig, not a turkey. I do make one accommodation—I buy no-nitrate bacon.

A native tomato provides the ideal balance for the salty bacon. The two flavors marry between slices of toasted bread, and with the attendants of fresh lettuce and mayonnaise, produce a flavor beyond the sum of its parts. It creates a gourmet meal, the perfect bite of sweet, salty, smoky, and tart, juicy tomato. It tastes like summer, and even more delicious to me, because I won't have another one until next year. With my first bite I close my eyes and sigh, "Mmmmm."

One early August day, a bin of native tomatoes at our local market triggered my annual BLT craving. Large and red, I tasted the sweet juiciness even as I held one in my hand. All winter, the pale-colored tomatoes contain hardly any juice, and their insipid flavor makes me wonder why I bought them. A good tomato should taste tangy and sweet at the same time. If you bite into it like an apple, the juices should run down your chin and drip all over your clothes. The succulent tomato flavor should explode in your mouth, even if you close your eyes. In the winter, if I closed my eyes and bit into a tomato, I would have no idea what I was eating.

My friend's husband, Don, made the best BLT I have ever eaten. He started with toasted, high-quality white bread, no whole wheat here, and buttered it liberally while still warm. Then he spread a generous layer of mayonnaise over each side, far more than I used. Next, he added four slices of perfectly cooked bacon, nitrates and all. Never too hard or too soft, he found the ideal spot in between. Add crisp, fresh, green lettuce, thick slices of fragrant, native tomatoes, and another layer of bacon before the final slice of buttered and "mayonnaised" toast. When I took a bite, the juice, butter, and mayo ran down my chin, and I closed my eyes in ecstasy. I have never tasted one as luscious since.

The tomatoes I bought at the grocery store, although native, did not burst with the flavor of summer, and neither did my BLT. It didn't satisfy my BLT longing. But the next day, my neighbor left an oxheart tomato—heart-shaped, and as big as a man's fist—on my doorstep. Meaty inside, it smelled of sun-drenched tomato essence, and it whispered, "BLT." How could I refuse?

22 Hours

"One day on Prudence is better than one day anywhere else." That's what Joe Baines said when I saw him at the ferry dock in Bristol the morning I went to Prudence Island for one steaming hot day, not even twenty-four hours. I trudged from the car to my friend Judy's house. Maybe this was a waste. Why come for such a short time? Then I slipped into the cold bay. The salty water washed over me and cooled my body to a comfortable level again. Even after a refreshing swim, the relentless sun drove me in search of a shady refuge.

I could have stayed home, avoided an hour-long drive each way, and slept in my familiar bed, and yet, I chose twenty-two hours on the island. I shared a spectacular sunset and a glass of wine with friends. If I had been home, I would have whiled away most of the day in my air-conditioned living room, and I would have spent all of it alone—no human contact, no conversation. Some days I'm happy without company, but I had a hanging-in-space, about-to-fall sensation that often follows my transition from intense family time to intense solitary time. I left my to-do list undone, but I spent time with friends. I absorbed the tranquility of Prudence as I sat on the porch writing, watching sailboats on the bay, and listening to the lap of water on the shore. It provided the renewal I craved.

Now, home once more, I sit on my screened porch and look out over my backyard, a soft breeze ruffles about me, and I listen to the silence. In this moment I try to float once again in the bubble of Prudence Island. It blocks the outside noise and allows me to see the world through a magnifying window. There exists a serenity on Prudence unlike anywhere else. I still hear birds sing, surf sweeping the rocks, and occasionally the hum of a lawn mower, but the filter of distance and the bay cushions the island, muffles the noise and frenzy of mainland life. It fosters stillness in my mind and quiet in my soul.

I hear the birds sing when I sit on my screened porch in Chepachet, and I find quiet in my surroundings there too, but I don't feel the same peace within me that I do on Prudence. Things on my to-do list yell at me in Chepachet, but I don't hear them on Prudence. There, my mind wanders back to my childhood, when my sister and I filled summer days with swimming off the rocks or playing with friends, and nothing pressing intruded on our minds. Do I still carry that quiet with me now?

Here, at home, cars drive down the road faster and more frequently. Even without traffic, the quiet I hear differs from that on Prudence. I listen, searching for the peace that I tried to carry home. Abruptly, the insistent whine of a chainsaw disrupts the landscape of sound around me. My bubble pops. I hope I can catch a ride on another and continue my journey into the tunnel of my mind. I dream of living on Prudence, and maybe one day, that dream will come true.

Dreams

The sign was painted white on red,
Across from the rolling sea.
"Reduced for sale," is what it said,
But I heard, "Come look at me…"

Walk along the clamshell beach,
Breathe the tang of sweet salt spray,
Return at night with sun-kissed cheeks,
Whisp'ring waves will end the day.

There is a rhythm to the tides,
A compelling ebb and flow,
That fosters peace in island life,
Brings balm to my aching soul.

Not all embrace the island's call,
Feel the lure of its commands.
A puppeteer, it moves the strings
To guide my feet, wave my hands.

The sign was painted white on red,
Across from an ocean view.
"Reduced for sale," is what it said,
I heard, "I'm waiting here for you."

Leaving

"Don't go yet." "Why don't you stay longer?" I hate leaving when it involves someone I love. Leaving, like letting go or saying goodbye, can lead to a period of grief. When I see my grandchildren either at their home or mine, I hate the moment of parting. I know it means facing a long span of time when I won't see them, because they all live far away. I'll miss their triumphs and their struggles, greeting them when they wake in the morning, and saying good night at the end of the day.

Once I am home, I am grateful to return to my routine, sleep in my own bed, and have quiet time for writing, but missing them becomes acute again. I try to keep the door closed on my longing to see them. Gradually, I readjust to being apart, and time and distance temper my grief, until another visit reawakens it.

Endings resemble leaving. They can make me sad and lead to regrets, but they exist tangled up with things I don't regret. Leaving a job has its own trials and can result in a stretch of grief. When retirement precipitated my leaving, the grief of no longer feeling useful and needed lingered, similar to what I felt when my children left the nest. But when I imagine taking a different path, I must accept not only leaving behind the things I regret, but also letting go of things or people that I love. I try to leave regrets in the past and accept that I am where I am based on decisions I made, both wise and imprudent, because even the poor decisions had some positive outcomes, and even the good ones had flaws.

Vacations seem to be long when I look ahead to them, but short when I return home and look back. They peel away into the past, barely leaving a ripple, like water flowing around a rock, sending undulations across the narrow passage of time away, and resuming its smooth flow in my cushioned writing chair. I don't want vacations to end because I will miss all the wonderful things unique to where I have been—scenery, food, and new challenges. On the other hand, I am happy to return home and settle into a spot of warm comfort, shaped to my body like a worn slipper. Nestled in a comfy chair I wander through my mind, and the clarity of vacation moments gets blurred by the recurrence of the mundane, and I wonder, did I go there? Or did I dream it all?

Treading Water

The wind has shifted, bringing a welcome change. I've been treading water for the past week trying to stay afloat in the confines of one air-conditioned room. I fight air conditioning like some churchgoers fight changing their pews. I try to cool the house with the evening breeze and button it up against the noonday sun. However, this past week the soaring temperatures coupled with high humidity, holding hands like inseparable lovers, has left me wilted. I feel like I've been living in an oven with a pan of water inside to create moisture and help bread dough rise. I don't function well, and I succumb to the charms of air conditioning.

I walk early, work briefly in my garden, then go into hiding. I put my life on hold. I stay in one spot, like treading water, to keep cool and move around as little as possible. Even the effort of using my brain seems too much.

I took my grandson to Prudence Island when he was ten. He swam like a fish, but the responsibility of keeping him safe weighed heavily on my shoulders, so when he swam from the rocks to the raft, I stayed in the water with him. He jumped off and climbed back on over and over again, laughing and shouting with another boy his age. I swam to the raft, but stayed in the water, going nowhere, my arms and legs in constant gentle motion, staying afloat, but not making progress. If I had tried to tread water for an hour without purpose, I would have tired and retreated to the rocks, but that day I focused on Ethan, watching his every jump into the water, and feeling relieved each time his head surfaced. I am not a strong swimmer, but I was convinced my hovering presence would keep him safe. I put my day on hold until he swam back to shore.

A series of events have put my life on hold. I have not moved from my hovering spot, treading water, waiting for I don't know what. I am trying to decide what comes next, make decisions while I sit alone in my one air-conditioned room, sleeping under a ceiling fan, waking to my coffee and routine of the morning, but making little progress, or am I? Maybe I progress with everything I do. I spent time with my grandchildren, I visited Prudence. What do I add to my life, to fill it with joy and purpose? Travel? Writing? Adventure? I want it all, but how? I need to stop treading water and swim.

Be Present

Yoga teaches us to be mindful, present in the moment, and if the mind wanders, to bring it back to focus on the breath. I begin most days with a short yoga session, and if my mind roams, I try to guide it back to the breath, but I don't always succeed. Some days I go through the movements automatically, without paying attention. The familiarity of the routine numbs my awareness in yoga, and in life.

Life becomes ordinary as I live it. I see the same things every day and follow the same routines until they melt into oblivion and become invisible to me. I spoon sugar on a grapefruit, hungry for the satisfaction of tasting sweet, but if I concentrate on the grapefruit without sugar, it tastes sweet as well as sour. Its flavor sparkles on my tongue, waking my taste buds. When I let go of my routine even briefly, I find refreshment and renewal when I return.

I can easily lose sight of the beauty and wonder of small moments, unexpected blessings, and ever-present gifts. I take them for granted; I cease to see, hear, or smell them. This morning, I hear the Phoebe; her clear, unrelenting call cuts through the chorus of other birds like an insistent child who craves attention. If I pause, as I stand on my screened porch, and look with eyes awake with awe, I can watch the Phoebe suspended in midair as she catches bugs on the wing. Like a hovercraft, she flies in one place, and an unsuspecting mosquito falls victim to her patience.

I begin my day deep in thought, the silence woven in between the unheard song as my mind puzzles on a problem or struggles with a decision. But if I focus, I can hear two Phoebes, their pitch slightly different, but their conversation intense. They answer each other—parents planning how to teach their children to fly? Newlyweds seeking the perfect spot for a home? Or lovers, one courting the other, in hopes of finding a partner for their winged journey?

If I listen, in the distance I hear a backup choir singing, the shrill call of the Red-bellied Woodpecker, and the melodic voice of the Wood Thrush. I hear them around the corner of silence yet lost in the noise of thought. A car speeds by, oblivious to the birdsong, disrupting the quiet. Are we cars? Zooming through the space between the notes, focused on our destination and heedless of our surroundings as we go about the endless busyness of the day?

I don't want to be a car; I want to be in the moment, like a child focused on an immediate instant of fun, not what happened yesterday or what tomorrow will bring, or what else he should be doing. Time spent each day being present, pausing if only momentarily, releases the constraints that dull our senses and allows us to see what exists before us, previously ignored. I can breathe in the stillness and peace that cuts through the distant blue; I can listen to a speck of silence with a mighty sound. I hear it now, unseen, as I sit and write.

Summer's Gift

S queak, squeak, the swing creaks as I gently rock my feet, heel to toe. The cool, early morning air wraps around me as I sip my coffee and listen to the birds waking and singing their good morning songs. Their daybreak chatter sounds bright and friendly as they start their gossip chain for the day. Their calls and my whispered breath, with an occasional comment from the swing, create the only ripples in the sea of quiet. The sun opens its arms; soon its light will yawn over the trees and touch my knees. I sit and allow the silence and peace to soak into my body and bones.

My wooden bench swing hangs in the shelter of a long, narrow porch enclosed by screens. It offers protection from bugs and rain, although it can't escape the heat of a still summer day. A story above the backyard, with no entrance except through the house, it feels like an airy cave of safety. Wind chimes hang on one end, and the deep, resonant tones vibrate on the slightest breeze, but today the air lies still as a sleeping cat, curled in a puddle of sunshine.

I have my breakfast and my first cup of coffee here in the summer. When I still taught school, I woke early on the first day of summer vacation and carried coffee, a book, the phone, and chocolate to the swing. I pulled a table close and took a large pillow to cushion the arm and the chains as I sat sideways. A little small for stretching, my knees stayed bent. I used the table in front of me as a launch, pushing the swing into gentle motion. I read until I slept and then I woke and read again, restoring my soul.

Sometimes I sit and look out at the woods. It provides a place to reflect on the day, to watch in wonder as a doe and her fawn come to eat fallen pears, a retreat to hold a lover's hand and share a kiss. It offers a sanctuary to think, to mourn, to talk, to celebrate, occasionally to sleep, and most of all, to be. At the end of a hot summer day, I sway on the swing as light fades from the sky, and listen to the birds say good night, their tunes now gentle and hushed. I used to hear Whip-poor-wills but now they have gone.

As darkness creeps through the screens, I refrain from lighting a lamp. The twilight makes conversation safe and thoughts free. The crickets and cicadas add their background buzz to the evening serenade, and the swing squeaks a lullaby as troubles of the day float on the gentle motion, spilled from my mind into the space of night. They cease to poke at me, not gone, but resting. The fire-flies blink Morse code between the trees. I drift on the gentle noises of the night, the wind, the crickets, and the birds, softer, softer into sleep. I miss the Whip-poor-wills.

Loneliness

$\mathcal{I}$ am alone but not lonely this morning. Alone and lonely live in separate rooms of the same house. Alone goes out and works in the garden, talks to the flowers, enjoys a morning walk. She listens to music and sings along, makes plans with friends and family, and savors cooking whatever she likes. Then her sister, Loneliness, crawls out of the attic room where she lives in darkness. She sneaks up and punches her fist with all her strength into her sister's stomach, leaving her rolled in a ball with her arms wrapped around herself so she won't come apart.

Loneliness remains a constant companion, and yet at times, she sits quietly sleeping, hibernating like a bear in winter. I am often alone, but being alone does not necessarily result in loneliness, and I can be lonely when I am surrounded by people. I enjoy solitude and following my own rhythm. I like the serenity of writing, or working in the garden, of communing with my own thoughts. I relish quietly reading or walking the beach on Prudence Island. It all seems peaceful, until the loneliness bear wakes from her nap.

Some people roar at solitude, find it unsettling, painful, a constant pressure on their minds and hearts. Why, I wonder? Are we hardwired to be with other people? Or do we learn the skill over time? Can we train ourselves to be at peace when alone? Am I hardwired to be an introvert, or did I learn it in my childhood when I had few playmates?

Solitude runs through my life like a river. Sometimes it whispers over the rough edges of my being and soothes them. It becomes something to savor and to choose, allowing the freedom to do what I want to do, responsible for no one else. Although I treasure solitude, I also long for companionship after my family visits, when Loneliness uncurls from the corner, and sits beside me.

I have days when Loneliness pokes at me, and I feel less of everything—less peace, less belief in myself, less value as a writer, less, less, less. Yet, if I open the gate to my mind and walk through, if I wander its paths until I connect with my writing brain, and then I sit and write, the time quickly passes. An hour gone, two hours, three, when I'm writing I lose myself in the story; the characters keep me company and soon I have written myself out of loneliness. My pain empties into my notebook, and though not yet completely healed, in time it will be. Even writing for fifteen minutes helps oust loneliness from my soul.

We all need a listening ear to stem the tide of loneliness. Writing provides a bridge over the loneliness river that flows through my life and threatens to capsize me; it offers a moment to breathe. Still, I accept that there will be times when Solitude once again slips from my grasp, and I hold Loneliness instead. Then I will write.

Alone

You are the specter that waits for me,
Filling the shadows where I cannot see.
Hiding in closets and under the bed,
Sitting at dinner when nothing is said.

I work in my garden all through the day,
Share tea with a friend, and yet you still stay.
A weekend in Maine, a trip to the shore,
Seeking adventure and things to explore.

No matter where, or how far I have been—
I return home to your endless din.
You squeeze my heart in an unyielding fist,
You drain my soul of its most recent bliss.

As evening descends, you slither round me,
Depleting my space and the air that I breathe.
I open a window to fragrant spring air,
But when I turn 'round, you're lingering there.

My family arrives here from far away,
With their hugs, and giggles, and love today,
But when they depart, and I close the door,
Your darkness looms, and consumes me once more.

The Silence Is Alive

I woke to the smell of brewing coffee today, so much more enticing on a chilly morning than on a hot steamy one. Our roller coaster summer has had some of both. The overnight temperature dropped forty degrees, deserting the nineties and funneling in the relief of the fifties. I left all my windows open overnight and my bedroom, which required the cooling breeze of the ceiling fan when I went to sleep, jars me awake with a cold nose and arms and legs burrowing to the foot of the bed where I threw the comforter the night before.

I pour a cup of coffee, and my hands wrap around its warmth. The first sip tastes like camping, when I leave the chilly, damp tent like a snake slithering into the open to find a patch of warm sun, and coffee tastes better than any expensive elixir. In the morning stillness, the sound of breaking kindling, and the snap as it catches the flames, pops from tent site to tent site. The cast iron frying pan clanks on the grill and the smell of frying bacon pervades the surrounding campsites.

No bacon sizzles in my kitchen, but the morning feels autumn fresh. I want to stretch out my arms and twirl! The smothering blanket of heat and humidity packed its suitcase and left town on the tail of the thunderstorm that raged through last night, scrubbing away the weight of pollen, dirt, and damp, and leaving a sparkling clean world. It departed with a promise to return soon, but I hope it loses its way and heads south where it belongs, midst the live oaks and the hanging Spanish moss. I long for a lasting visit of crisp, clear mornings that demand the heat from a mug filled to the brim with dark richness and allow for brisk, invigorating walks instead of slogs through soupy air that makes breathing difficult.

Even the silence is alive this morning. The air breathes in deep nourishing breaths, and the wren singing outside my window declares his stake in the day. A voice answers from deep in the woods. This morning, they sing an ode to joy, their voices louder, and more insistent. The wrens move on and a Song Sparrow picks up the tune. In the distance I hear honking geese. Will it be an early winter?

I sit in my writing chair in a sunbeam filtered solely by the trees. The air sings with the music of birds, the gentle movement of wind chimes, the sharp bark of a dog. Sounds normally too far to carry echo through transparent air that can see all the way to the ocean, without cloud, or fog, or particle of dust to interrupt it. I hear a motor from an unseen lake, a motorcycle from a distant street, carried on the breeze that flows like a mountain stream around me, cool, refreshing, alive.

I am alive this morning. The bracing air breathes life into my bones and my brain. Today, thoughts flow more freely, and problems appear less daunting.

Today I am ready for an adventure, to hike, to bike, to climb a mountain, even to mow the lawn. It summons me to get out of my chair. I sat enough the past few days of searing, unrelenting heat. The world waits. What should I do? A long bike ride calls, "Leave the unmown lawn, the unweeded garden, the unwashed floor. Go! Move! Do something worthy of being alive! See this day through the eyes of discovery, the joy of a child, the song of a bird who sings because he can." What shall I do because I can?

Listen

When I step outside myself, I listen better. I listen with my body, mind, and soul. When I absorb the sounds around me, I am no longer me, I am the origin of sound. On Prudence Island, I become the breath of Prudence—the birds singing in the morning stillness, the silence of fog, or a hot summer day, the rhythm of waves. I wash along the shore, touching abandoned shells and become the tide flowing over the rocks. I am the wind off the bay, filled with salt and brine, I am silence steeped in solitude.

I absorb the sounds, the smells, the taste of Prudence, tucking them away to sample and touch when I get back home. I stand in the middle of my yard in Chepachet and the warm sun reaches deep inside me and finds the seeds of Prudence, the childhood days stored somewhere in the visceral memory of my mind. It releases the lock, and the memories tumble out. In the quiet of this one moment—no cars, no lawnmowers, only a faraway finch calling to his neighbor, and the insect sounds of summer—I close my eyes and I am there. For one moment, I am on Prudence again. Then the breeze caresses my face, like a lover saying goodbye, and Prudence vanishes. A car guns its engine, a dog barks, a lawnmower roars to life, and Prudence slips away, back into its hiding spot, until an unexpected sound or smell opens the lock again.

Some days I am my writing; I pour myself into the pen and become the words on the page. The rhythm and the rhymes are mine, and I am them. My mind flows like a river, listening to the cries of pain or songs of joy—

Some days I hear no voice of me,
I write the concrete wall I see,
I cannot climb its hard, rough height,
I cannot carry my words in flight.
Listen, listen, the white noise begins,
The sound of water trickling in,
I lose my rhythm, and
The washing waves echo like tin.
Then notes from a flute in a faraway place,
Calm my mind on a note of grace.
I write, I listen, I walk with the air.
The night now covers me everywhere.
I listen, but my mind wanders far,
How do I write to reach a star?

Healing Notes

I drove to Providence as the rain sluiced over my windshield and my stomach knotted in distress. My friend languished in the hospital. Her gaunt frame faded day by day. I felt helpless, beyond comfort, and prayed she would find the strength to fight this battle, and win. My pain came with unbidden tears, until they matched the torrents outside.

I needed a distraction, so I pushed aside my sad thoughts and let my mind wander a forgotten path, to a time before my children were on their own.

On an afternoon much like this one, I came home in pounding rain that worsened an already stressful day teaching high school. When I walked through the door, I found my son Adam, a high school senior, standing at the counter inhaling a snack, to feed his constantly ravenous six-foot two-inch body.

"Hi Mom, how was your day?"

"Miserable," I said. "Several of my classes were noisy and disruptive. They wouldn't settle no matter what I tried. I'm exhausted."

He stopped eating and kindly asked, "Is there anything I can do?" I asked him if he had time to play the piano. He often did this on his own, and it relaxed us both, him by the playing and me by the listening. I'm certain it also provided a welcome distraction from the homework that awaited. I settled in a comfy chair by the piano and closed my eyes. When he began to play, I knew what I would hear without asking, and he knew what I wanted him to play, without asking.

The familiar first four notes of Pachelbel's "Canon in D" sounded beneath his fingers, and the tightness began to disappear as my muscles and jaw relaxed. I allowed the music to wash over me like soft waves on the shore, swirling around me, and dispelling the tension from my body and soul. He played it through twice, and as the notes faded in my memory, I realized I could hear them now.

The same first four compelling notes of my favorite restorative music emanated from my car radio. I listened, and they worked their faithful magic. The knots in my belly loosened as the melody played, and the clenching in my shoulders eased. I arrived at my destination with my worry and despair tucked away for now, surrounded by this moment of spirit-healing peace.

End of Summer

The insects strum outside my window; after a brief respite from the heat and humidity, summer edges back today. The sounds around me change as summer melts into autumn, hanging on to the last puddle of warmth before cool nights descend and require me to close the windows and grab a jacket as autumn sneaks through the open door. Spring mornings create a cacophony of sound. The birds sing their joy for sunny days and winter past. They return from vacations far away in warmer spots and greet their neighbors with tales of their adventures. They sing heartfelt notes of courtship, and the music rouses me at daybreak every spring morning.

Now, in September, I wake to the endless buzz and chirp of crickets and cicadas; the incessant sound goes on without pause into the middle of the night. But the songbirds remain silent. Their courting has ended, the chicks have fledged, and those who travel prepare for their long flight. I sit by the open window in my sunroom and hear only an occasional crow, calling his displeasure as another steals the pear he had chosen for breakfast.

The hummingbirds' buzzing dives will soon leave my garden too, and it grows quiet as the color pales and the late summer flowers fade and drop to the ground. Tall phlox produced its pink and white parade for almost a month, but now the flowers slip away, one by one, leaving behind clusters of green seed pods—the vessel for spreading them willy-nilly around my garden. I don't mind. When the heat and drought of summer have wilted other perennials, phlox soldiers on, an extravagance of color without boundaries. After the lingering phlox blossoms drop, and I cut all the stems, the garden shouts one more hurrah before winter.

Chrysanthemums will soon explode in a last flush of color, masses of vibrant hot pink flowers with golden yellow centers, like the last seconds of a sunset when it sinks into the bay in a fiery ball, spread across the beds. They replace the calming blue delphinium with their bubble gum pink that announces, "It isn't winter yet." The chrysanthemums bloom until winter's first killing frost, surviving the light sprinkle of cold or even snow, that might arrive in early November. They shine a final spotlight of color in the garden before it fades into sleep. Even if I do nothing, the garden will grow quiet and still, fold away the green mantle and replace it with a crunch of brown leaves, a crispy blanket against the cold, until the warmth of spring wakes it once more.

In winter, I long for those first warm spring days, but now, with another blast of heat on the horizon, I long for the clear, unblemished days of autumn, when basking in the midday sun feels like rich chocolate, soaking into every pore. Although fall lurks in the shadows, the insects still hum, the night lacks a nip to send them scurrying to their lairs, and they sing on through heat and damp, ending when the late September chill finally arrives. A motorcycle zooms and a plane rumbles overhead, interrupting the subdued insect concert, then stillness reigns again. I listen to the crickets and make plans for a dwindling summer day.

A Day to Write

I look out the sunroom window and watch the light sidle through the trees. Rain falls and leaves cling precariously to the skylight. My fleeting thought—I want to wrap myself in a cocoon of ideas and allow my writing mind to wander where it will, without restriction, then transcribe those meanderings on paper.

Some days my mind rambles while I watch, spontaneously writing a story or a poem, and some days it waits for inspiration like still morning air. On other days my mind hits a wall papered with my to-do list. All wandering ceases, except for scanning up and down the list and making a plan to get it done. The door slams shut on my creativity as with a stormy gust of wind and I hear my long-ago parent's voice, "Get your work done, then you can play." Accomplish the chores on your list, then you can write.

Sometimes my writing mind finds a chink in the wall; long methodical tasks, like mowing the lawn, allow it to escape the bonds of my to-do list, even briefly. As I walk back and forth across the yard, with no thought required except to turn before I run into the stone wall, my writing mind sneaks in and says, "Come with me," and I do. Often I have to go back over my thoughts, like a tall patch of grass that needs a second pass with the mower. I want to tamp the ideas into the earth of my brain, so when I finish this chore, I can dash into the house and write furiously, remembering the ideas that skipped unencumbered across the blank screen of my mind.

My thoughts take flight, launching from the page. I sit in the cockpit with my pen, and the engine fires up, but even when I am cleared for takeoff, I don't always know where I will land. Though I have a destination in mind, I don't know the route, or I begin one way and find it blocked. If I allow my mind and pen to fly unrestrained, they will take me to unexpected places. Rivers of emotion swirl around me and I pause for a swim; other times I judge the water too cold or the current too strong and I skirt the river with plans to return when I am stronger.

I try to focus on my writing, but part of my brain impatiently taps its foot, waiting for me to put down my pen and get busy on the important stuff. I remind myself that this moment, right now, is important too. If I follow the route that unfolds, perhaps I will reach the place where unrealized dreams live, like my dream of publishing another book, but that won't happen unless I pick up my pen and begin.

Fall

In Search of Ice Cream

"Ice cream! There's ice cream! Hey everybody, there's ice cream over here!" No one listened to my call.

A few days after my youngest son got married, we toured Jamestown with Adam's new wife Becca and her out-of-town family. We strolled along the Rhode Island coast on a sunny, unusually warm October day, and I alerted everyone to ice cream. The rest of the crowd focused on taking family pictures. I, on the other hand, tried to encourage them to get their priorities in order—ice cream first and then pictures.

My youngest son, my baby, planned to launch himself out of the nest and move to Missouri. I definitely needed ice cream, but no one else understood.

I inherited the ice cream gene from my mother and grandmother. Despite her belief in the importance of balanced meals, Mom could shop all day, and frequently did, with nothing more nourishing than an ice cream cone or two. Chocolate was her favorite, while my grandmother preferred coffee. I've never met a kind I didn't like, though if I had to pick one flavor, it would be coffee too. I could easily eat it for breakfast, lunch, and dinner. Do I? No, I have a well-developed parent living in my brain that tells me ice cream alone does not represent a valid meal. I have to eat my vegetables before I have dessert. Although sometimes I think of my mother, then skip everything else and go straight to ice cream.

I much prefer locally made ice cream to the commercial varieties you can buy year-round in the grocery store, and I can probably list fifty ice cream shops within an easy drive of my Rhode Island home. When I travel, I am on high alert for local ice cream parlors that make their own ice cream. I have found them from Bar Harbor, Maine, south to Pensacola, Florida, west to Portland, Oregon, and numerous places in between. My family says I have ice cream radar, and like a cold-seeking missile, I home in on it wherever I visit. If they make ice cream, I will find it.

My dad sold ice cream in his general store every summer. My childhood memories of summer fun, security, and the best place to be in the world, are all connected to ice cream. When my life feels topsy-turvy or off balance, I turn to ice cream and allow the sweet flavor of coffee, ginger, or lime to slide down my throat in a rich cascade. Its smooth creaminess freezes my distress on the spot, so I can pluck it up in one piece and put it away for a while. My enjoyment as I eat an ice cream cone gathers the splintered, painful shards of my troubles like a magnet, and I feel myself growing whole again. The ice cream fills not only my empty stomach, which I hardly notice, but also the dark corners of my soul, and I see myself righted, back on balance once more.

Island October

The wind has shifted overnight, hurling itself across Narragansett Bay from the Northwest, and replacing gentle summer breezes with gusts that have the bite of winter lurking on the edges. The temperature hovers near forty degrees, and the air carries a bracing crispness as I begin my morning walk. The east side of Prudence Island has already watched the sun rise, but as it crests the trees that march across the apex of the island, the west side, where I am, still waits in shadows. Wasn't it yesterday that I traveled this road in shorts and a tee-shirt, hoping to finish my walk before the heat of the day? Today, bundled in gloves and fleece, I long for the sun to finally complete its arc over the trees and warm my corner of the island.

The high tide flings rowdy waves on the rocks, and one small dinghy rolls on the swells as they make their mad dash towards the shore. The waves provide the only sound I hear this morning, and if the birds are singing, the relentless pounding of the surf drowns them out. I see a seagull perched on a rock that peeks from the water, and he shrieks his morning thoughts. Is he sad to see the summer end, taking the visitors who might leave behind an occasional stray quahog, or does he prefer to have solitude return and the bay to himself? His voice overrides the surf and soon another call answers, even more raucous than his.

As my walk bends away from the water and the buffer of saplings and underbrush muffles the crashing waves, I listen, waiting to hear the first morning calls of the resident songbirds. But I hear only the wind, a distant plane, and one solitary crow. Perhaps the songbirds have already begun their journey south in search of warmer places to sing.

I came to Prudence to help my friend Judy close her summer house for the winter. I feel melancholy when we say goodbye to carefree island summer days, and sometimes the warm October sun tempts us to linger for one last swim and postpone closing for a few more weeks. Evening temperatures that drop into the thirties reinforce the wisdom of the decision to button up the cottage. The frosty night reminds us that winter will soon embrace this little island and without heat or insulation, the disaster of frozen pipes will be real if we don't complete the winterizing process.

When Judy and I board the ferry the next day, we leave her house all tucked in for the winter. Though I will revel in future snows, my mind will wander ahead to May, when balmy spring days entice us to return to Prudence Island, songbirds serenade my morning walks once more, and the bay beckons to us for our first chilly swim.

Pemaquid Point

Don your wool socks,
Wrap up tight,
The Pemaquid wind is awake tonight.
It riles the waves
And spooks the gulls,
But for myself,
To sleep it lulls.

Autumn Leaves

Some years the leaves set my yard aglow with fiery color in October; other years, leaves bypass those brilliant hues and fall from the trees brown and crisp, like a thick crunchy carpet that totally obliterates the grass. I wait until the trees sport naked branches to rake—I only rake once. Fortunately, I have maples in my yard. They relinquish their leaves all at once, unlike oaks that hang on to theirs through the winter, dropping a few at a time. Today, a dense, red and orange leaf blanket covers the lawn; I'll corral most of them, but I will allow some to cloak the garden beds and keep them warm and snug through the winter.

I love the crunch of dried leaves against my feet, and raking leaves the old-fashioned way, with a real rake, satisfies my soul in a way a leaf blower never can. A rewarding fatigue fills my arms after a day of raking and dragging mounds of papery leaves into the woods on a blue plastic tarp. On most late October days, the end-of-autumn dried leaf smell mingles with smoke from nearby woodstoves. Today an unseasonable warmth makes it feel more like early September than late October, so no one has built a fire. Still, I enjoy the smell of fresh air and the earth preparing for winter.

When I tuck myself into bed tonight, my limbs will be ready for the satisfying sleep that follows fatigue from physical labor. In the spring the sound of birdsong accompanies my garden tasks, but no birds sing today, and I enjoy the quiet and occasional rustle of my rake. I clear beneath the pear tree that has grown as tall as its neighboring maple, although its more fragile boughs would not support the weight of adventurous boys who climb to the top, as the maple did.

I look up through the branches and remember the August days when unripened pears covered the ground. These Seckel pears, good for pickling or making jam, most often feed the deer. August dusk draws them from the woods, the scent of ripening pears the signal to leave the security of their hiding place and venture into the open, where they can feast on this late summer delicacy. The mother eats with one eye on her two fawns, her ears perked to hear the approach of danger. The little ones graze, oblivious to all but pears and their mother, trusting her to keep them safe.

Occasionally, they abandon the treats and succumb to the open space in the yard circled by stone walls. They chase each other like boisterous children, back and forth across the lawn as fast as they can run. The wall provides a boundary and they turn and run back with such joy I can almost hear them giggle and shout, like my boys playing tag with their friends. When a sound alerts the doe, she lifts her head, testing the degree of danger. If she feels it threatens too closely, she gives a warning snort and runs into the trees, leaping a low spot in the crumbling wall that leads to their safer wooded home. The fawns quit their game of tag and follow their mother without a backward glance at the pears that remain on the ground. Even their gangly young legs carry them over the wall with grace.

The next morning, frost coats the ground. My hands grow cold on the rake after an hour, and I decide to stop, but not before I catch a whiff of smoke from a neighbor's woodstove floating on the breeze. Ahhh, now it smells like October.

Autumn Gift

Silent fog enfolds
Colors wrapped in gray paper
Opened by the sun

My Writing Chair

Can a room have a personality? The sunroom where I write, in what I refer to as my writing chair, does. I love this room. Even on gloomy days it appears cheerful. Filled with light and plants, scattered books, an unfolded blanket, singing radiators, the smell of lemon blossoms, and paper loons flying aimlessly over my head. The room where I hold my grandchildren and show them birds, zoom cars, and play rummy. The heartbeat of my house, where I go to find comfort and rest, to share tea with a friend, and to write.

I didn't initially create this room for writing, I created it for plants, and for me. When my parents bought this house in 1966, it had an enclosed summer porch. They had it winterized, and when I moved here more than forty years ago, my children used it as a playroom, but over time they grew and moved away. I acquired a variety of houseplants so I could garden in the winter, and the plants eventually occupied so much room, I didn't have a place to sit, so I remodeled.

I added skylights and a garden window that provides a wide shelf for plants where they're surrounded by glass, even overhead. I painted the walls a pale blue—the color of a summer sky, hung pictures, and added a blue and yellow flowered couch and matching glider chair. Three older chairs, along with a few tables from our Prudence Island house, complete the furnishings. It provides plenty of room for my plants, friends, and for me.

The transformed room now radiates peace and offers a safe place to spill my soul as I search for direction in life. I pick up the broken pieces and put them back together, one at a time. Sometimes the songs of George Winston play in the background, sometimes merely the wind and rain. The random beating of water on the skylight accents the silence, though the sounds of boys' rowdy soccer matches still live concealed in the walls.

When I began my first book, I returned here again and again to write down random thoughts, and over time, without planning or intent, the glider became my writing chair. When I am here, my mind settles in to write. I designed the room to be a place of comfort and replenishment, to give rest to my soul, and my mind feels free to wander wherever it chooses.

I often compose first drafts as I walk, talking to a small recorder, but I compiled and edited my books as I sat on the sunporch. I have tried to write in other rooms, but my mind keeps pulling toward the light and inspiration of this room and this spot.

The glider also carries my burdens, absorbing them into its soft, comfy cushions; it cradles me in its white wicker arms. I begin almost every day here, coffee cup in hand. I say a prayer of gratitude and watch the day come to life, as the sun clambers branch by branch over the trees, and the songbirds stretch their vocal cords for the day. I hear a Phoebe's insistent call, or a finch's delicate chirp. The outside world surrounds me, but I sit here safe from the elements. I often indulge myself by curling up here to read, and I have sobbed with grief and pain over the death or illness of a friend. I have written my soul and body onto the pages of my notebooks, and wandered through the recesses of my mind in search of peace. I have waited for God's hand to find me and lift me from the depths of sorrow up to joy again. I look forward to seeing it, like an old friend when I have been away, and like a faithful friend, it waits.

Grief

❦

Within the fields of joy, the seeds of grief are planted. The more we feel the pain of grief, the greater the love that nurtured it. My mom died in 2005, four days after Thanksgiving, and I still feel the pain of that loss, especially when I begin my Christmas baking. She planted the joy years ago that spawned this pain. As a child, I climbed on a chair and stood beside her, learning from her and helping her as she made cookies or cakes. My mom and I enjoyed each other's company, and most of all, we loved to bake together.

I am familiar with grief and its sneaky ways. I've seen my parents and grandmother die and grieved for my favorite aunt. I have lost three longtime friends, and I've held the hands of seven friends when they buried their husbands, parents, and sister. Grief will not be ignored. You can push it to one side, you can build a wall to keep it out, but it doesn't work. Grief haunts you and infiltrates your defenses when you least expect it.

Grief has no season; it pursues us, skulking in the shadows waiting for a moment of weakness to pounce. We can face it as it comes, or we can turn our backs and ignore it. But then it returns, gathering strength with each added loss, until like a hurricane tsunami it sucks everything within us dry as it recedes, and comes pounding back with a force that crushes and drowns us under its weight.

My friend Sandy died suddenly. I had known her since fifth grade and lived next door to her as a teenager. A few months later, my college roommate and friend died after a long decline with dementia, and then COVID. Grief overwhelmed me, faded the color from the sky and the energy from my body. It drew the air from my lungs, and I sat in silence. Books remained stacked and unread; the weeds grew in my untended garden. My writing pen sat idle, waiting.

Why does it matter? What is the point? The questions haunted me. Draining, emptying, the tide receded, leaving the beach strewn with sharp rocks and seaweed, covering the sand with debris. How could I walk? Find the path? Where would I go? I didn't know, and so I sat, heavy limbs burdened by the weight of grief and loss. The light of friendship faded from one corner and then another, like dominoes, falling, breaking one by one. Spots of darkness merged and left me in silence.

One day I thought I would drown in my grief, no help in sight, no life ring to grab, and my feet floundering as they sought the bottom. Then—my son Adam called. I talked; he listened. I couldn't see the way back, but he could. He gave me a resting place and I caught my breath.

He didn't throw me a lifeline and pull me to shore. He simply said, "I see a piece of driftwood floating by, can you reach it? Do you need me to swim to you?" "No," I said as I grabbed the board and started kicking. I still couldn't touch bottom, but I no longer searched to find it.

The shore remained far away, still a long swim, and the water was over my head. But I could keep going. I needed to know someone saw me and recognized my struggles. Now that I knew I had help, I stopped flailing wildly, my strength renewed, and I no longer felt defeated. I saw the shore. I saw hope. I could keep going. I swam through the night, and the next day I reached the shore again. I began to write, and I knew I would find my way back.

Ultimately, grief remains a solitary journey. No one can feel exactly what we feel or miss the things we miss. No one knows the lost relationship except the person who faces the emptiness. Yes, some common threads exist— aching pain in your heart and a gnawing sense of loss. Everyone responds differently. Some push it aside and forge ahead, some cease to function. I think most of us land somewhere in between.

This I know: if I don't allow myself to grieve and walk through the pain, if I shut the door and turn my back on grief, it will return like a monster let out of its cage, angry and more intense, at the most unexpected moment. I need love and a listening ear when I grieve and although they don't erase the pain, if I know someone sees me and recognizes my struggle, my soul can rest. I can heal, and find joy and peace again.

Fading Light

Day after day of endless gray,
Weeping skies hold sun at bay.
Swirling fog hides the view,
Swathed in silence, sound gone too.
Like a puzzle frayed and worn
Pieces jumbled, edges torn.
The curtain parts, a light shines through,
"Do you remember?" "Yes, I do."
Winsome smile, at last it's you.
Years of friendship kept in balance
Reading poetry, searching science,
"Have you been here before today?"
"Have you been here before today?"
"Have you been here before today?"
The blue is swallowed by the gray...

Words Like Water

I don't mind the solitude of writing, but sometimes my mind tricks me and disappears when I want it to be present. It goes off on a rant to attack the bills to be paid, floor to be washed, or the lawn that needs mowing. I want to call it back to me and say, "Sit here and tell my pen what to write," but it can't be bothered. It has retreated to a world of concrete blocks, and I want to sit in a field of tulips and inhale their phantom smells.

Some days the words flow through my pen like water flows within the banks of a river. The bank curves, the water follows, and yet the water carves the bank further into itself. Water can be an irrepressible force. It created the Grand Canyon, it washes away buildings, telephone poles, and trees. It whispers and soars depending on its mood. I have walked the ocean shore in silence, when the water rested in meditation as quiet as the fog that hovered on its surface. I have walked when waves broke on the sand with such power I continued to hear the constant roar even when I couldn't see it.

Water changes lives; it feeds the food we eat or drowns it in excessive abundance. It rocks the sailor to sleep or tosses him like a tiny cork and spews him from its mouth. It caresses the bathers' feet as they walk along the shore or comes crashing beyond its limits to demolish a cottage by the sea. It has the power to destroy lives, and it soothes the soul with gentle music flowing over the rocks, unchanging, ever present through the night.

Words are like water. They can carve a place in history. Words can soothe, touch the listener in tenderness and carry him to a place of peace, or rile him to anger. Words can be spoken with love and with hate. They can whisper or shout, bring comfort to the soul, or tears to the heart. They can quench thirst and drown pain. They can wash away grief or cause it, incite a fire in the soul or soothe as gently as a lullaby. Writing, like reading, offers the chance to experience life events again. When I reread a favorite book, the words sound familiar, but each time I read them a new door opens. I hope the words I write open the door and invite readers in; I hope they evoke joy and peace, and say, "You're not alone, someone else has felt that way too."

Grumble or Grateful

I have little to complain about and much to be grateful for in my life, and yet I often reverse the two. I get tired and cranky, grumble about the heat, having too much to do, not seeing my grandchildren frequently enough, the garden and yard that get ahead of me, a big house filled with unused "stuff," and longing to live on Prudence Island.

Still, I can turn all that around and be grateful for my old farmhouse home, well built, cozy, and welcoming, with a sunroom that brightens the coldest winter days, and a screened porch that allows me to hear the first and last birdsong of the day—waking chirps and good night whispers. I have a garden that bursts with colorful, fragrant flowers from March to October, and I am still physically capable of mowing the lawn, weeding the garden, and shoveling the snow.

I often sit and read a book for hours, because I can. I'm free to choose. I write, and the floors go unwashed, or the grass grows for one more day. I can choose. My sons are successful and happy where they live and work. I can go visit them when I feel the pull to see them and my grandchildren. I can drive or buy a plane ticket. I have a friend who owns a house on Prudence Island, who generously welcomes me to visit, and if I really want to make the leap to live there, I can let go of my old farmhouse.

A week visiting with my grandchildren flies by; I can fill it to overflowing, treasuring every moment, or complain how little time I have with them. I can think of everything I left undone at home or let it all go. My day starts with joy and shared love instead of solitude. I say a silent prayer of thanks that I can be with them and they want to be with me. I can carry this lesson home with me. When I visit with friends, I can give my time and my presence without being tethered somewhere else.

I know I am never truly alone. I have friends who encourage me through my struggles and challenges, and a family I can depend on to help me if I need it. I am blessed with too much to be grateful for in life to waste time complaining. Instead, I can treasure and embrace every second, and be present. I can start each day with a prayer of gratitude for where I am, in this moment, and the life I have been given, before it disappears.

My Favorite Knife

The kitchen timer rings. I open the oven door, and a cloud of nutmeg-scented steam envelops my face. The Grape-Nut pudding sits in its water bath, awaiting the test of doneness. I open the utensil drawer in search of my special knife, but I can't find it. My practical brain says, "It doesn't matter, use a different one. It will work as well."

My heart responds, "I want the special one, it works best." It looks like an ordinary butter knife that would sit next to a dinner plate. The plastic handle, once a sunny gold, has turned dark okra. This knife possesses a longer, thinner blade than my other stainless knives, perfect for determining if a pumpkin pie or baked custard is cooked. Its increased flexibility also makes it work better for loosening a cake from the pan, especially angel food or sponge cake.

Its physical attributes make it work better than my other butter knives, but I consider it special for a different reason. It sat on our big oak table every night on Prudence Island. I have a matching fork, but no spoon. I use the fork too, and though perfect for testing baked potatoes, it doesn't excel at its chores as the knife does. Part of a set given to my parents as a wedding gift, the knife and fork have survived for over eighty years, since 1940. The initials EHK still march down the handle, as precise as my mother, Evelyn Herlein Kaiman.

An invisible thread ties to both and draws me back in time, through the kitchen door on a cold evening, to the welcoming smells of dinner cooking on the gas stove. My mother lifts the pot lid on the simmering potatoes and uses the fork to determine if they have finished cooking. Then she mashes them with the green-handled potato masher that now lives in my utensil drawer. I think of my mom when I use the fork and the masher too, but for some reason, I hold the knife most dear.

While my brain and heart continue their argument, I see my mother slipping the special knife down the tall side of an angel food cake pan. Up and down, each stroke separate from the next, so the cake emerges unmarred by the knife blade, still a continuous flow of golden brown edge. I've tried it with other knives and always succeed in making marks and rips in the delicate crumbs. She mastered that persnickety job and seldom disturbed the golden-brown crust that encased the tender cake. I am more impatient and sometimes leave behind several knife gouges in the cake.

I close my eyes and see her use the knife to test Grape-Nut pudding as she bends over the open oven door. It slides in and comes out clean. Now I want to use that knife to test my own Grape-Nut pudding, and it has gone missing. I refuse to accept a substitute. That knife is experienced, it has tested hundreds of puddings, released as many cakes from their pan prisons. It has frosted cupcakes and spread peanut butter on bread in one smooth flourish. It contains the years of my mother's cooking and love wrapped within its aging handle and still flexible blade.

I rummage around the silverware drawer, searching in the back and under the salad tongs. "Yes!" I shout, when I find it concealed beneath the collection of serving utensils. I insert the knife into the custard and when it slides out clean, I remove the fragrant pudding from the oven and place it on a cooling rack. I will wash the knife and put it back in a special corner of the drawer, unhidden, where I can find it the next time I need its unique talents.

November

The shadows stretch long this late November afternoon, and I amble through the crisp air under a cloudless blue sky. I walk to the top of the dam where a biting wind strikes my face. A Great Blue Heron spreads his wings and glides gracefully across the pond, leaving one rocky perch for another, a safer distance from me. I wonder if he will return to his original spot when the echo of my footsteps fades.

Walks and bike rides this time of year reveal hidden treasures. The trees stand devoid of leaves and the woods offer views of their secluded ponds that remain indiscernible on summer day meanderings. Although most of the leaves now carpet the ground, occasionally I come around a corner to the unexpected sight of a maple tree that holds fast to all of its autumn glory, and vibrant red orange leaves still cling to its branches. I pause and drink in this final gift of nature before colors fade, the world grows cold, and bike rides cease until spring.

When I arrive home from my walk, the birds chirp noisily, reminding me that the temperatures have plummeted and the feeders sit empty. I put blocks of suet in the hanging wire cages and birdseed in the tube feeders. Three feeders hang outside my kitchen window, one for thistle seed, which the Goldfinches love, and two for mixed seed, which everybody else enjoys, especially the squirrels.

We have had a cold snap this week; I'm grateful that I picked the last of the lingering summer roses. They now sit on my kitchen table, sharing their cheery color and sweet perfume. Last night's killing frost, and the two inches of snow we had the night before, left their fellow, overlooked blooms curled and brown. Most Novembers find my garden beds securely put to sleep for the winter. I have given them a generous drink, if needed, and some food to see them through the dark winter days. I tidy everything, then I wait patiently for the arrival of the first snowdrop blossoms, usually under the melting March snow. This year, traveling and family commitments meant that in mid-November, my garden beds remained in disarray, and I felt restless and fidgety. I feel the same way when I walk into my bedroom to sleep and find the room all higgledy-piggledy and the bed unmade—unsettled instead of peaceful.

A cold wind blows out of the Northeast, plunging temperatures into the twenties each night, unseasonable for this time of year, and also keeping the daytime temperatures unusually chilly. These cooler days no longer make me wish to be clearing gardens or munching fresh picked apples out in the orchard; instead, I want to be cozied up in front of the fireplace with a pot of butternut squash soup simmering on the stove and apple crisp bubbling in the oven, filling the house with the spicy fragrance of cinnamon and brown sugar. Thanksgiving will be here soon, which means apple and pumpkin pies, squash rolls and cranberry sauce. My thoughts stray from gardening and move on to holiday preparations.

I know I will not plant any more flower bulbs or groom my gardens this autumn. Fortunately, the daffodils and crocuses, snug now in their winter homes, forgive my inattention, and like faithful friends, they will return in the spring, with their brilliant colors and sunny dispositions, despite my November neglect.

Laughter

I pour my coffee, curl into a comfy chair, and open a book of daily meditations. I repeatedly find the topic for the day relates to my emotions or struggles of the moment. Today's entry refers to mistakes; that could apply to me most any day. We all make mistakes, which offers an opportunity to forgive ourselves, family, and friends. I try to view them as gifts of joy, because they prompt me to laugh at myself. Not lapses that result in pain to others, but the small day to day foibles that inconvenience us. They can give us a reason to laugh, and I take full advantage of those moments. I sip my coffee and think about past *faux pas*. The list is long…

Like the morning I reached for the orange juice but couldn't find any in the refrigerator. *That's funny*, I thought, *I don't remember finishing it*. I shrugged and opened the cupboard in search of oatmeal to cook for breakfast. Right beside it sat the orange juice.

One day, when I taught junior high, a student said, "Mrs. T., why is one heel on your shoe brown and one blue?" I looked down and discovered I had on one shoe from each of two different pairs of navy blue sandals. Another time a student said, "I like your purple shoes, Mrs. T." It surprised me to find I still wore the purple flip-flops that served as my warm weather, indoor only, slippers.

When I taught at Toll Gate High School, the arrival of a computer for each classroom pleased all the teachers. During my free period, I wanted to see if a local Dick's Sporting Goods store had the soccer equipment my son wanted for Christmas. Being new to computer workings, I entered "Dick's" in the search engine. Imagine my shock when it wasn't sports equipment that appeared on the screen. I couldn't turn the computer off fast enough! I shared my adventure with the department secretary and we both laughed, as did all the teachers she told. The story generated laughter in the lunchroom for days.

I make soup at a meal kitchen every week, and one day, I intended to sprinkle black pepper over the sautéing vegetables. However, the plastic lid fell off, and I dumped in the entire contents of a large jar. After we all stopped laughing, we put the vegetables in a colander, rinsed them with water, and put them back in the pot. Now whenever someone makes a mistake, I say, "Don't worry. Remember the pepper?"

I closed the small green book and put it back on the bookcase. I realized that the time I wore two different shoes happened thirty years ago. Not much has changed—I still make mistakes, and they still make me laugh. I reached for my cup and took a moment to give thanks for my blunders and the joy they can bring—I wouldn't laugh nearly as much without them.

A Cactus Story

T hanksgiving fast approaches and the air hangs heavy
with November. This morning as I sit in my writing chair I hear the rain on the skylights, a comforting
background to the radiator singing beside me. Though
still dark outside, cactus blooms brighten the room: red,
pale pink, orchid, and peach. The cactus next to me swells
with promise. Tiny, almost imperceptible buds cling to
the stem ends. They have another month to fatten and
grow, until they burst into exquisite, hot pink blossoms on
Christmas. They began as a small cutting from a friend,
and now I have three huge, hanging cactus plants.

I look up from my notebook and study another plant.
At some point, when still tiny, I must have put a second
cactus in the pot. Or perhaps the cuttings, waiting in a
glass of water, tangled their roots together, and I planted
them as one. Now, I see two different colored buds, one
red and one peach. I have three enormous peach-colored
plants. I guard them fiercely but share them freely. They
originated with one from my mother. When she died, I
brought the small cactus plant home from her apartment.
I had never seen it bloom in all the years she had it, and I
didn't know what color to expect. I wonder if it felt lonely,
the sole cactus she possessed, but when I brought it home,

it became part of my indoor garden, surrounded by other plants, and its beautiful peach flowers appeared. I have shared cuttings with multiple friends, and I grew one for each of my sons.

All my cactuses have a story to tell, a connection to someone, and when they bloom, I think of the story and remember the person who gave each one to me. The bright red ones, alone in one large pot, and sharing space with a peach companion in another, came from the wife of my sons' band teacher twenty-five years ago. I wrote many mental letters to Mr. Pandolfi, telling him how much his example and guidance meant in my sons' lives. But the words never left my mind to land on paper. Now it's too late.

The largest plant in my cactus garden boasts an orchid throat within its pale pink blossoms. Its flowers cascade gracefully on branches weighed down by the profusion of blooms. Forty years ago, my husband's uncle gave me a cutting, one slip in a glass of water, from a plant that belonged to his deceased wife. Over the years, he became a second grandfather to my children. Did I ever tell him how much we all loved him and appreciated his place in our family? I hope he knew, but I can no longer tell him in person.

Mary, my friend and support when I taught at Toll Gate High School, gave me the orchid pink cactus. We worked together for thirteen years, and when I retired, I said I would keep in touch, but I've seen her only a few times in the past fifteen years. Though I think of her, we don't call or write or stay in contact, as we promised.

The cactus plants start blooming around Halloween

and continue, one by one, to open through Thanksgiving. Then, after a pause, three hanging cactuses provide the grand finale of Christmas blossoms. A friend who sang alto with me in the church choir forty-five years ago gave me that one. Have I ever told her how much her constant friendship through the years meant to me?

Cactus plants are like people—each beautiful in itself, each with its own time to bloom. If I sat in my sunroom all day, every day, I could watch the flowers unfold in slow motion, opening one at a time until the whole plant bursts with a unique, bright color. As one cactus fades and the blossoms fall, another has already begun to replace it as the star of my cactus garden. The parade continues until the final flower shrivels and falls at the end of January. They provide three months of continuous bloom, and then they rest, until the cycle begins again next year.

Some of the plants have morphed over the years, absorbing color from the one beside it—in one pot the pale pink has more dark pink highlights, in another red tinges the peach. Like us, the people we meet, the places we go, and the friends and decisions we make change us. Even though we start as a gene pool unique to us, the world molds us into who we become. The cycles in our life repeat. We have times when we bloom with joy and abundance, and times of sorrow, when the bright colors in our lives fade, until we rest and gather our resources to begin again. Some of us grow larger, bloom longer or more brightly, and some of us swell with promise never to be realized. We give up, allow the world to knock us down, or early tragedy sweeps us away. When offered the chance to come into full bloom, we have the potential to radiate joy and share it with the world.

Every cactus has a story, like us. My mother fills my mind when the peach cactus blooms, and I think of other individuals when "their" cactus blooms. The plants remind me that though cactus plants live on, blooming every year, people don't live forever. I don't want to miss the chance to tell them what they mean to me. I'll write notes to my longtime friends—today.

Early Snow

Six inches of snow fell one late November day, not the light fluffy December snow that brings thoughts of snow globes and Christmas cards, but a heavy, wet snow that mixes with rain and shovels like cement. It didn't frost the branches white, but left them dripping wet instead. The morning began cloudy, leaden with unfallen snow, and gray with penetrating cold. A walk on a clear, cold day in December feels invigorating. I can see my breath in the crisp air, and as my walk lengthens, I grow warmer with each step. But November brings a different cold, and November snow smells different. It wiggles itself into the nooks and crannies of my two-hundred-year-old house and the dampness in the air soaks my soul, making it want to retreat inside to hot soup and a fire in the hearth. It demands an extra layer against the bitterness and saps my body of motivation. "A book and a cup of tea, please," responds my body when I ask it to take a walk. I promise to reward it later with tea by the fire—after the walk.

The next morning the snow calls to me and says, "You have to shovel." I had hoped to bypass shoveling and let the sun's warming temperatures do the work for me, but it stayed cloudy and didn't warm as much as predicted, so though it's early November, I already had to shovel my driveway. The lingering snow releases me from other outside chores. I can't finish raking the leaves that cover my lawn or drag the pile I raked on a random warm day into the woods. I can't finish cutting back the remains of my perennials and tidy the garden. I feel like I've been let out of school early.

Maybe there will be another unseasonably warm day between snowfalls, and the yard will beckon to me, or the garden will send waves of guilt flowing over me from my neglect, but more likely, as I wait for snow to melt and wet ground to dry, it will be spring before I pick up my rake again. I had also hoped for one more bike ride in the sunshine on a warm fall day, but I think that window has closed. I will bring my bike into the cellar for its winter sleep and push my driveway reflectors into the ground before it freezes solid.

Today a ribbon of pink and mauve flutters deep behind the trees as the sun tiptoes up and slowly wakes. I wonder if it needs a second cup of coffee like I do. Today I'll start my Thanksgiving baking—after I walk. The snow tosses shards of cold into the air like frozen confetti and they settle around me as I set out into the frosty morning.

Letting Go

*A*s a memory keeper, I have a natural tendency to cling to things that have sentimental value. The abrupt destruction of my dad's store when I was eight triggered our move from Prudence Island to Barrington—a life-changing event. My dad got a job on the mainland and, for a year, only came home on the weekends. My sister went to school in Bristol and traveled with him.

I loved school on Prudence; I felt safe and accepted. Everything changed when I walked into the fifth-grade class at Primrose Hill Elementary school in Barrington. I no longer had the freedom to pace myself and spend more time on what interested me. When I made a mistake, the teacher yelled at me in front of the class for not listening or following directions. I shrank into myself, and my love of learning and school faded into a shadow of what had been so much a part of me; pieces of me fell away. Is that why I hold "things" close?

Transitions create rough spots in writing and in life. Bumpy transitions in writing makes reading the story like riding a bicycle over cobblestone streets. It throws everything off-balance. Children struggle with transitions. It upsets their inner ear of consistency, and they complain, refuse to move, or even have a tantrum. The adult world finds this unacceptable, and though I may not act out my distaste for change or transition, it doesn't mean I feel it any less. I turn my distaste inward. I pour my heart out on the page, and sometimes my tears come too. I stuff my feelings with ice cream and chocolate instead of letting them be. Maybe I would be better off if I stamped my feet and yelled.

I'm not good at downsizing mentally; I'm sentimentally attached to many things. I feel like I'm peeling a giant Band-Aid, taking skin along with the tape—a painful process. I think, *How can I part with this? I remember...* And I am off on a convoluted journey back in time. I have read numerous books about how to minimize "stuff." Whether specific items like clothing, or miscellaneous articles, which fill my house. I have eliminated some of both, but it barely scratched the surface of my possessions. I want to downsize my "stuff" while I can easily handle it, at least physically.

My instincts tell me to go closet by closet, drawer by drawer, room by room, but I haven't made much progress with this approach. I get caught in the tunnel of sentiment and tumble down the rabbit hole of remembrance, and the day disappears without my making it past the first box. I have a house filled with memories. My parents lived here before me, so many things belonged to them, or to my grandmother. They link to people who are no longer alive. I know these things don't contain the people I love. And yet, when I hold an article and turn it in my hands, I am holding something they treasured, and it transmits that treasuring through my hands to my heart. It triggers memories, tells me stories, and I cannot cast it aside on the rubbish heap.

I'm not worried about recent acquisitions. No, it's the ones tucked far to the back, the ones wrapped in memories and tied with a string of love that I find difficult to eliminate. Why do I struggle to discard things I'm not using? I feel attached to them, like I felt to the people who owned them. I see my mother in the dress she wore to my wedding. I remember my friend Shirley when I hold the blanket she made for my first baby. When I slip on an apron my grandmother made, I sense her standing beside me.

Boxes of unused items sit in my closet, but when I look at them, I see parts of me, and I get emotional when I think about discarding them. It tightens a band on my chest, and I turn away, move on to a different task. I read a book or wash the kitchen floor. Maybe someday soon I will be ready to open a closet door and begin. Maybe someday soon, I'll be ready to let go.

Lessons from the Ants

Our home is gone, they demolished it,
We need a brand-new place to live.
Where shall we go in the midst of this blast?
Where shall we go and settle at last?
We wander over the trail ahead, mount obstacles in our way,
It doesn't matter where we live, or if we arrive today.
All that matters is we find a home, where we can
   live together,
Though we may never own, or even live there forever.
A sea of black floats across the floor,
Its undulations hard to ignore.
It ripples and slides, moving as one,
The mass migration has begun.
They don't cry or weep in despair,
They pack no possessions and go anywhere.
Travel light, no bags for them,
Ready to move and begin again.
No old clothes, no sets of dishes,
Stay together, that's what their wish is.
No worries about which is best,
They build themselves a brand-new nest.
Their memories all travel along,
While they keep the beat of their marching song.

Why can't I move with the black ants' ease?
Why can't I be content to stop where I please?
Why can't I let go of being here?
Discover something new without fear?
But memories live in this house, my home,
They have kept me company when all alone.
If I move on to someplace new,
The memories I find will be few.
No shouts of laughter will fill rooms there,
The house won't exude love and care.
Four empty walls,
What will they hold?
Why can't I be like an ant—brave and bold?

Thanksgiving Day

The leaf design stipples the green linoleum floor as the wind blows and makes the patterns move in disconnected steps, stopping and starting to its own rhythm. As Thanksgiving Day dawns, I drift through the few moments of limbo between waking and sleeping, and the leaves form a dancing pattern on the floor of my mind; when the dancing leaves vanish, I am unable to fall asleep again.

I like to slide the turkey into the oven then go for a walk; the fresh air energizes me for the busy day ahead. The morning air of Thanksgiving whispers stillness—not a weather stillness, but a mortal stillness. Folks stay home to prepare Thanksgiving dinner, and my early morning walk remains quiet, uninterrupted by people or cars. I hear the sound of my feet hitting the pavement at a brisk pace and feel refreshing, cool air on my face. I inhale the scent of wood smoke as neighbors fire up their woodstoves or fireplaces in preparation for the company to come. Anticipation swirls around me; I imagine the fragrance from roasting turkey and pumpkin pie inside each house I pass, but the billow of smoke from the chimneys offers the sole sign of life.

By the time I return, the house already smells of roasting turkey. My mouth waters as I open the oven door to baste the browning skin and it triggers a memory of preparing Thanksgiving dinner for the first time in my married life. My out-of-town family would arrive before noon and I began preparations half asleep at 4:00 a.m. I didn't have skewers or kitchen twine to truss the turkey, so I pinned it together with safety pins. My solution sent my mother into gales of laughter when she saw it, and the shared giggles banished my fatigue.

This year my company will arrive later in the afternoon, and by then the mulled cider will add its fragrance of cloves and cinnamon to the roasting turkey. I peel the potatoes, butternut squash, and turnip so they will be ready to cook. I remember another year, when I was pregnant with my first child, and I had the vegetables peeled and in pots ahead of time. When my company arrived, I turned all the burners on high, but when the smell of burning vegetables permeated the house, I realized that I had forgotten to add water. All the vegetables got scorched. Although our tiny apartment kitchen had barely enough room to turn around, and a measly foot and a half of counter space, I had enough extra pots to redo the salvageable remains of the vegetables, except for the boiled onions (I put them in the teakettle). The finished vegetables still tasted delicious, although the onions cooked in the teakettle turned an interesting shade of dark gray. I laugh to myself and add water to all the vegetable pots.

Yesterday, baking squash rolls perfumed the kitchen and took me back to my island home where my grandmother baked bread every week. We had hot rolls for supper that night, made from extra bread dough. Smells often connect me to another time and place, because the smells of my childhood stay firmly rooted in my brain. They carry me away, and sometimes I can't even identify the smell, though it forms a direct link to another time. I have bittersweet Thanksgiving memories of my mom. Still, I treasure the loving memories prompted by the smells of Thanksgiving. I think of my three boys soon to arrive and wonder what memories they each cherish and carry inside, prompted by the smells of Thanksgiving.

Blueberry Glue

"Remember the Blueberry Glue Pudding?" asked Peter. My family remained gathered around the table after Thanksgiving dinner. Everyone felt pleasantly full, and no one wanted to move and break the invisible tie that held us fast. Even fidgety grandchildren stayed to enjoy childhood stories told by their dads and uncles. Although I usually tried to forget my cooking disasters, my three sons took great pleasure in remembering them in detail.

The Blueberry Glue debacle, precipitated by my boy's love for any kind of pudding, became a favorite family story. My youngest, Adam, though not yet born then, says that he has heard the story so many times, he feels like he experienced it also. One day, I found a box of potato starch in my kitchen cupboard, and I saw a recipe for blueberry pudding on the side panel.

I followed the recipe exactly, cooking and chilling it as recommended, and served it for dessert at supper that evening. The consistency resembled dried out wallpaper paste, perhaps a tad stickier, and the flavor, I imagined, bore a similarity too. I thought I had created a disaster, best put back in the memory cupboard and never mentioned again. My boys, on the other hand, deemed it a great success! They renamed it Blueberry Glue and even requested it in years to come.

"Mom, remember the Blueberry Glue Pudding? Why don't you make that again?" I couldn't bring myself to repeat what I considered a culinary disaster. In time the requests faded; however, it still holds a treasured place in our family lore.

Eric smiled as he reminded me of a wedding cake I had made. The finished creation sat on the dining room table, and I had shut the doors to ensure its safety. However, when I got up early the next morning, one door had been pushed open a tiny crack. There, reaching from a chair with her front paws resting on the table, stretched our calico cat Gwendolyn, lapping frosting as fast as her tongue could move.

"NOOOO!" I shrieked and roused my sleeping family, who came running to see what caused me to yell. I had to deliver the cake that afternoon, and I didn't have time to make a new one. I carefully removed a piece encompassing the area where Gwendolyn had been indulging her sweet tooth, filled the spot completely with leftover frosting and administered a little repair work to the piped borders. I swore my sons to secrecy, so when I finished, no one but the boys and I, and Gwendolyn, knew what had happened.

"I remember the only time I ever heard Mom swear." Adam's statement halted all conversation. My grandchildren's eyes immediately grew round. Nana swear? Impossible! As Adam continued, the events unfolded in my mind as clearly as a movie rerun. We had finished Thanksgiving dinner, and I decided to get an early start on the turkey soup. I put the turkey carcass in a large pot along with water, carrots, celery, onions, and seasoning, and let it simmer for several hours. Finally, I had a fragrant broth that would be the base for turkey soup the next day. Since I wanted it to cool quickly, I needed to remove the bones from the liquid. While the rest of the family peacefully watched football on TV, I took my big metal colander and put it in the sink. Then I poured the soup into it. It took a minute or two for realization to penetrate the turkey-induced coma of my brain, but when it did, I brought everybody running with my screams, and a few choice words, as I watched that rich, savory stock trickle down the drain.

I wonder why the best loved stories often grow from our mistakes. When the frustration has waned, do we find the whisper of humor that gives life and breath to the story through the years? I don't mind that my sons' favorite humorous tales hinge on my foibles. I know they recount them with love, and the retelling weaves a family tapestry that binds us together and reveals who we are. Thanksgiving provides the perfect time to be grateful for the blessing of our stories that begin, "Remember when..."

The Dishwasher

The dishwasher is invisible.
It nestles in the cupboard of nonexistence and hides its
    door in the hardwood floor
Patterned with spatters of winter squash soup.
It hums silently to itself, while the CD player sits
    on the shelf,
Singing the "Hallelujah" chorus with music and
    voices glorious.
It sees itself filled with dinner remains—soup bowls
    covered in orange stains,
Delicate wine glasses, and heirloom plates, cups now
    seeking their saucer mates.
It sprays soap bubbles to coat all the dishes,
Carrying clouds of steam with the dishwasher's wishes.
The china sparkles in the sun, the dishwasher's job is done.
The dishes rest in their plastic nest and wait to return to
    their cupboard home,
But the dishwasher stands alone.
A glass of sherry in her hand,
The CD changes and plays a brass band.
The dinner leftovers now put away,
The nest is empty, they've flown today.

The clatter of spoons and forks has gone,
Quiet plays a mournful song.
Emptiness now is all that's left,
The dishwasher moans in the quietness.
The birds eat suet by the windowsill,
And the dishwasher listens to hear their trill.
Gone from here, they all have gone,
What is my purpose, what is my song?
The dishwasher stands all alone,
Invisible here in her silent home.

I Am an Amaryllis

The light flickers through the amaryllis blossom. The sun has yet to crest the trees, but for a few seconds, as it continues on its path to the south, the translucent, orange-red petals glow with morning fire. The bulb had sat forgotten in a burlap bag for over a month. The roots had dried and begun to crumble, and I gave up hope of seeing it bloom. I thought I had destroyed it, but I planted my amaryllis bulb anyway, nestled in a cozy pot, with its head and shoulders visible above the soil. I gave it a drink and put it in the sun. I could almost hear a sigh of relief as it settled itself and began to grow. There were no harsh words or admonition, only grace and gratitude. For three weeks it sat with no visible change.

I decided there would be no blooms forthcoming. Then one day, I noticed the green leaves were a fraction of an inch taller than the day before. The initial growth took place hidden from my eyes—roots developed from the giant bulb, deep within the pot. And from somewhere inside, a green shoot worked to push its way to sunshine. Would there be a bloom for Christmas? Maybe not, but I had hope again. I knew it lived, and in time it would display a beautiful giant red trumpet. Despite my neglect, a spectacular invisible flower still dwelled inside that bulb.

Although conditions were not ideal, it continued to grow, and I put it out of my hurried mind and flipped the switch to patience.

The giant bulb contained all the necessary nutrients, except for an occasional drink, a ray of sunshine, and the small amount of soil surrounding it. I watched as the flower stem grew taller, and turned the pot to keep it straight, not always pointing towards the sunlight. It had two stems: clearly one would bloom, but I thought the other had been stunted beyond hope. I thought wrong again. Long after the first flower stem put forth four fire-engine red bugles, the second suddenly leaped towards the light. The tortoise transformed to a hare, and it bloomed like its sister, with four spectacular trumpets of red clustered on top of the stem.

I will learn from the amaryllis. Even neglected, it held life within. Beauty that needed only the smallest amount of nourishment to surge into the sunlight. My brain contains all I need to write, except for tools like a pen and paper, and an occasional infusion of enthusiasm and experience. The words I write hide within me, even when I leave them neglected, as the pen and paper sit idle. Then I walk, breathing fresh air and sunshine into the dark corners of my mind and the pen flies over the paper. My heart and my soul run across the page for anyone to reach. Once started, they keep going like roots, reaching deep into the soil, searching for every morsel of nourishment. When the amaryllis has bloomed, it will send out leaves to store food for the next season, when hope will bloom again.

My mind sits in a cozy spot, wrapped in cleaning, cooking, and shopping as I anticipate the arrival of my family for the holiday. The rooms will soon overflow with shouts and laughter, and there will be no room for cobwebs. In all the time alone, you might think my brain would write, while my hands clean. But writing stays embedded deep inside me like blossoms in that amaryllis bulb. I'm waiting for quiet, time, and space to let it grow. Lengthy to-do lists overwhelm it right now. While I keep working, my writing mind rests, waiting to burst with words, but not today.

The books simmering inside me poke the surface, like a garden of bulbs getting ready to break forth in the spring. But if I trample the emerging stems with impatience, if the frost of criticism freezes the buds, there will be no blooms. They need time and patience, sunlight and rain to grow and flourish and bring joy to my garden. We all need time and encouragement, the warmth of positive thoughts, and space to be. Bitter words offer no nourishment to the soul, nor do judgmental thoughts. I am a writer, and I will write, but I can only be the writer that I am. The amaryllis bulb will never be a daffodil.

Being read and published are not what make me a writer. Even if my amaryllis never blooms, it stays an amaryllis. Two red petals gently flutter, vibrating with the radiator's heat, like the edge of a flag in a whispering breeze. I will let go and be an amaryllis.

Winter

Shortbread Memories

The snow falls in slow motion. Puffy moist flakes frost the trees and cloak the world in silence. I sit quietly while tears slide like silent snow down my cheeks. It's almost Christmas. I've decorated the tree and baked cookies. Soon my house will swell with laughter, love, and hugs. The sounds will vibrate, playing the notes of Christmas in every room.

The lingering aroma of shortbread cookies floats through the house, conveying the essence of Christmas, sweet, rich and simple. They smell of company and love, but also of loneliness. The empty house aches with the lost sounds of children playing and soft conversation over the shared tasks of Christmas baking.

As I watch the snow, I hear the padding of small feet and squeals of laughter, as three little boys push their chairs to the counter to help with Christmas cookies. I envision my mother and I baking together in my growing-up years, or in later years, enjoying each other's company as she sat at the kitchen table while I baked. My mind goes from one to another, the ghosts of memories float around me, and while happy for the coming celebration, I am sad for what has gone, never to return.

Those boys with mischievous smiles and sticky hugs

are grown and have wives and children of their own. Now I am Nana. My mom, my sons' Nana, is gone. She loved Christmas and the preparations it entailed. As the boys got older, she would disguise their presents so they couldn't guess the contents inside, and she often arrived on Christmas morning before they woke, especially when they became teenagers. As she got older, and no longer cooked, she still enjoyed the food, especially dessert. Though she would say she was "full up" at the end of dinner, as she drew her hand in a line across her forehead, when I asked if that meant no room for dessert, she invariably said, "Oh, I have room for dessert."

The sweet smell surrounds me. The sweetness of a baby's fingers wrapped around mine, the sweet strains of love when the family gathers at last in one place. The simple ingredients—butter, flour, and sugar—reflect the simple pleasures of Christmas. It's not the expensive gifts, but the quiet of a candlelight service, the softly falling snow, and the comfort of everyone together, sleeping under the same roof, as the house sighs in contentment, and so do I. It feels different, it smells different, it sounds different when I am alone, but now the scent of shortbread fills all those unoccupied spaces, and I embrace the sweet memories. I realize I am marching relentlessly towards being "full up" with a dinner someone else has prepared, but I will always save room for dessert.

Nibble, Nibble Doubt

We all deal with negative voices, some spoken by other people, and some whispered from a secret recess of our mind. I don't usually have a problem overcoming other peoples' voices when they doubt my ability to accomplish my goal; it spurs me on. However, my own negative murmurs of doubt cause me angst and weigh me down so I can't move forward.

When I decided to run a marathon, I had no doubt that I would finish; I made a training schedule and I followed it. Did I run as fast as I had hoped? No. But did I finish? Yes. Several years later, I wanted to complete the MS 150 bike ride to raise money in honor of my son's mother-in law. I had to ride seventy-five miles for each of two consecutive days. One doubter gave me a ten-dollar donation with these taunting words, "It's worth ten bucks to see if you can do it." The unspoken message? "I'm betting you can't." Little did he know that his challenge kept me going when I fell three miles into the second day, banged my head and left a good portion of one hip, one elbow, and one knee on the pavement. There would be time to acknowledge the pain later. I wouldn't give him the satisfaction of saying, "I knew you couldn't finish." I got back on my bike and rode until the end.

When I taught middle and high school, I wrote two grants and both times other teachers questioned how I would be able to accomplish them. They emphasized all the problems they could see ahead of me, but I didn't listen. I didn't worry about the reasons I couldn't do it, or challenges I might encounter. I made a plan and followed it. When each grant period ended, I had completed every item on the list.

So why do I find it hard to finish writing my current book? I want to make time to write, but I have a long list of excuses that prevent me from writing and completing the book I started five years ago. I tell myself to pick up the pen, put it on the paper, and keep it moving. Then Doubt silently stalks me. It steals in unnoticed, infiltrating the nooks and crannies of my life. It whispers in my ear, "You can't write, no one will want to read your book." It leaves me ragged and full of holes, like a moth-eaten wool sweater forgotten in the closet.

Sometimes Doubt takes gulping bites until everything I thought I had built crumbles under its ravenous assault. I doubt my decisions, I doubt my perceptions, I doubt me. If something doesn't work, it must be my fault. I must have done something wrong. It chews away at my confidence, my determination, my acceptance, my peace.

In the instances where accomplishing my goal helped someone else—raise money for MS, provide programs that would benefit the students and the school community—the negative voices originated in someone else's head, and either they motivated me or I could tune them out. Now they originate in my mind and constantly torment me. I can't tune them out and instead of inspiring me to move forward, they beat me down.

I love to write. I need to stop worrying and wondering if it is good enough and write until I finish. Then I can work to make it better. If I send my desire for perfection to the compost pile, my writing mind can soar. My pen can fly unhindered by the critical voice of Doubt. I am enough, my writing is enough, the joy I find in words is enough. If I believe in myself and do it, the rest will follow; the book will end, and my heart and soul will be on the page. I hope the reader will be in a better place after reading it, and I will be too. I will finish it for them, and for me.

We can all choose to leave the baggage of doubt behind like we shed winter clothes in the spring. I cast off my baggage of doubt by giving thanks for this moment. I am where I want to be, grateful to be alive and writing.

Christmas Circuit Overload

Every Christmas my circuits get overloaded. I'm not referring to an excess of Christmas lights that blow a fuse, but the circuit overload that goes on in my brain at Christmas time. My children delight in sharing holiday stories that begin, "Remember the year that Mom…." Admittedly, I am an easy target for their humor, being a bit absent-minded in the Christmas frenzy. I always respond the same way, "My circuits were overloaded," and as a single parent of three boys, my circuits often did get overloaded. Through the years, the things I forgot have become the things they remember.

I had a habit of buying Christmas presents early and tucking them away, in order to spread the expense over a longer period of time. One year, my two young sons wanted and needed warm boots; their sneakers were not sufficient for playing outside in the woods on cold winter days. About two months before Christmas, I saw a sale on the perfect boots. I bought them and hid them high on a closet shelf where I knew the boys wouldn't stumble on them by mistake.

Christmas morning, we gathered around the tree to open gifts, and Eric and Peter were delighted with everything they received. About a week later, as I cleaned and put away the remnants of Christmas, I discovered a familiar bag high on a closet shelf. When I looked inside, I found two brand-new pairs of boots. Annoyed by my forgetfulness, I gave the boots to the boys. The late arrival of the gift didn't bother them. They tried them on, bundled up, and went outside to play.

Then we had the year of the watch. My son, Adam, asked for a pocket watch the year he started high school; they fascinated him, especially if the back opened so you could see the workings inside. I searched everywhere for a pocket watch, but they were all priced way beyond my budget. Then I stumbled on a watch sale months ahead of Christmas. Thrilled, I bought a pocket watch and put it away in the back of my bureau drawer where I knew he would never unearth it. Christmas came and went. A few weeks after Christmas I found the watch and thought, *I don't want to give it to him now, I'll wait until his birthday*, which happened to be in February. I put it back in the drawer, but his birthday came and went, and I forgot about the watch. When I came across it again, I decided to save it until next Christmas; he still wanted the watch, and he didn't know I had it. Christmas and his birthday came and went, and I continued to forget the watch. Finally, Christmas his senior year in high school, I wrapped the watch *first*. That year, Adam's two older brothers, who didn't know about the pocket watch, decided he should have a watch for college. They lived in different states and both researched watches. Unbeknownst to the other, each picked the style he thought would be best. On Christmas morning, Adam opened a stylish wristwatch from his brother Peter, a high-tech watch that did everything, including tell the time, from his brother Eric, and a pocket watch from me. We all laughed at my ongoing absentmindedness, and Adam was still elated to receive the pocket watch, albeit a few years late.

Years later, Christmas approached, and I knew my whole family would soon arrive. My sons, with the addition of two girlfriends, one wife, a grandson, my sister and her husband, and my mother would be here. If I didn't get busy, I would be wrapping gifts on Christmas Eve in the midst of my family.

I sat down in the living room one evening to begin my project. I needed a plan and devised my own personalized assembly line. I gathered all the gift boxes I had saved from previous years, spread them out on the floor, and matched each one with a present. As I placed the cover on every box, I labeled the top with the name of its recipient. Then I piled the whole collection next to my chair and started wrapping one box after another. As I wrapped, I complimented myself on my efficiency. Rather than putting a gift in a box, wrapping it, putting the ribbon and tag on it, then starting the whole procedure over again, I had streamlined the process. I finally finished with the wrapping stage, and on the opposite side of my chair stood a tall pile of festively wrapped packages. Now I could complete the last step of adding a bow and a tag to each box.

As I reached for the first present, I realized that in my self-satisfied frenzy of wrapping, I had covered the names on all the boxes. I couldn't face unwrapping every one to find its owner, so I proceeded, adding ribbons and tags to the best of my ability. I tried to remember what each box held, although many had similar shapes and sizes. I finally finished and placed all the gifts under the tree. Christmas morning they surprised everyone, especially me.

Peace

_P_eace, peace, peace. The words sing in my head as background music, quiet and contemplative. Sadly, in this season of peace on earth, peace often eludes me, in the troubled world and in my life. I am easily caught up in my to-do lists. Cookies and scones to bake, gifts to buy and wrap, and my car to pack and drive for eight hours to be with my family. How do I find a fragment of peace? How do I touch it and dwell within it daily?

This winter morning, I find peace as I creep in sleepy caution down a long flight of stairs. I hold the railing on one side and the wall on the other to steady my not-quite-awake steps. The smell of coffee drew me from my bed and as I descend the stairs, I hear its inviting burbles and bubbles. This time of year, my morning begins in the dark. I flip on the overhead light in the sunroom and wait for the space to fill with its glow. I snuggle into my favorite chair and hear the companionable hiss and clang from the radiator as it scours away the night chill. I wake slowly, stretching with the sun as it sends out an advance guard of light before making its first appearance of the day. I hold fast to meditation time, and then write for fifteen minutes. I start the day being present, centered, not scattered.

I look up to the opposite wall where I see a picture I painted almost twenty years ago—an impressionistic field of flowers along the water's edge. Some days I feel the sand in my toes and I hear the lap of waves as I walk through the prickly color to the waiting shore. Other days I see a still lake where I could paddle my canoe to the edge and sit amidst the sweet fragrance, keeping company with birds and butterflies hovering nearby to drink the nectar. My mind slows, the chatter quiets, and I remember how the brush felt in my hand and how the painting came to be.

I had finished teaching for the day and arrived at my son Adam's apartment for dinner, two hours ahead of him. When I opened the door, I found an easel holding a blank canvas with a chair next to it. A Post-it note stuck to the canvas said, "Fill me." On the table beside the chair sat an assortment of paints and brushes, a jar of water, and another note that said, "Use me." An old shirt of my son's was draped across the back of the chair with a note that said, "Wear me." His 6'2" frame compared to my 5'4" meant the shirt would protect my clothes from paint splatters. Next to the easel, a second table held a CD player and a note that said, "Play me."

I set my bags by the door, and with a smile on my face and tears streaking down my cheeks, I pulled the shirt on over my clothes, pressed the play button, releasing soothing music by Enya, sat in the chair, and picked up a brush. I dipped it first in the cup of water provided, then into the blue paint, and I began. Two hours later, when my son walked through the door, I stopped and declared my painting finished. It remains untouched by brush or paint since that moment. Whenever I see it, I feel Adam's gift of peace, and I smile.

Today I think of seeing my grandchildren and all of my family soon in Baltimore for Christmas. As this day begins, I envision sitting in church on Christmas Eve with my sons. I imagine hearing "Joy to the World" and "Silent Night," and remember the peace nestled between the notes and the words that tell of a humble birth. I find peace elusive in days of hectic activity, but I let go of the rush and say a prayer of gratitude for this day, because in gratitude, I find peace.

Happy New Year

New Year's Day, 2018, I looked out my sunporch window, and the sun glinted on footprints frozen in the snow—the remnants of our Christmas celebration. Though it started as frozen rain, it soon turned to white fluff, bringing the longed-for gift of a white Christmas for my three sons and their families, including four grandchildren ranging in age from three to fifteen, who had traveled to Rhode Island. The afternoon of Christmas Day, they played in the snow that had fallen that morning. Footsteps crisscross each other in abundance, and I could hear the echoing squeals as children flung themselves into the snow to form snow angels. After building a snowman and the inevitable snowball fight, they returned inside, rosy-cheeked and happy to chase away the cold with Christmas cookies and hot chocolate.

The temperature plummeted after Christmas, and the snow remained frozen in place, a reminder of children playing, hugs and kisses, "I love you Nana"s, and my family once again gathered under one roof. I look forward to it every year, as it is often the sole time we are all together. We take turns hosting, and the years we celebrate in my home, where my boys grew up, feel extra special to me.

I settled back into my solitary days, but the scattered

toys and unmade beds reminded me that for a little while, noise and love filled the house again. We laughed together, and sometimes cried. We played games, sang carols, opened presents, ate yummy food, and enjoyed each other's company. I listened to the radiator sing and heard the parting goodbyes, as the footprints in the snow snaked into the woods and disappeared.

In 2020 a raging pandemic prevented our family from being all together in Rhode Island again, and we divided our Christmas celebration. On New Year's Day, 2021, I received the news that my friend of sixty-five years had died suddenly. Later in the year I attended the funeral of my college roommate. Christmas of 2021, my family again celebrated together, and I felt blessed to have them all return to Rhode Island, with the addition of one more grandson. Although the joy I felt at my family's arrival tempered the pain of my friends leaving this world that year, when January 1, 2022, dawned, I happily said goodbye to 2021.

I begin this New Year with hopes to live each moment with joy and gratitude.

I have much to be grateful for every day, even simple things, I don't need extraordinary. I sit in my writing chair and the rose geranium beside me releases its seductive perfume when I brush against it. Like all friends, it needs attention. I neglected it during the holiday bustle. Now the leaves droop and some have turned brown. As we all do under stress, it needs a fresh outlook on life. I'll trim away the brown leaves and soak it in a tub of warm water to ease its tired branches and breathe new life into its fragrant leaves.

I remind myself that every day, not just January 1, offers the chance for a new beginning. When a new year dawns, though I might feel the lingering pain the previous year brought, I can hold tight to the moments of joy it also brought and carry them into the new year. I can treasure time with my family, grateful for their love and support. I can be open to God's creative guidance, and pray that my words and actions will consistently foster love, peace, and joy. I will be grateful for all that I have been given, and I will continue to write.

Taking Down the Christmas Tree

The Christmas tree stands naked. I hate taking it down as much as I love putting it up.

Before Christmas, the living room vibrates with pending excitement. The smell of baking cookies lingers into the evening as I lace the lights through the branches of the tree and wait for the bubble lights to heat. I take out the boxes of ornaments: a shoebox filled with satin-covered balls, red, green, gold, and white, and the square box with a removable cover where birds live. My mother had a collection of feathered birds for her tree, including a bright red Cardinal; I had a Cardinal too, and now my mother's and mine nestle in the same plastic bag inside the box. Each of the others, a tiny wren, a pheasant, and a collection of unknown varieties, has its own plastic bag to protect the feathers. On top, sit the glass birds, with wire-like tail feathers, that my dad clipped on our Christmas tree when I lived on Prudence Island. They still send me into flights of nostalgia, and though some of them have lost their tails, I clip them on anyway.

As I hang each ornament, the anticipation of family time and celebration grows. Each ornament triggers a new memory and thoughts of the Christmas to come. I study the ornament my youngest son made in elementary school from a tiny photo of him sandwiched between two pieces of red, heart-shaped construction paper; it sparkles with glitter. One side of the heart has an opening cut to fit the picture, like a jam-filled sugar cookie, and a loop to hang it protrudes from the top. The picture makes me smile. I remember Adam as a little boy, and imagine seeing him soon, with his own little boys.

For two weeks I turned the tree lights on every night, and enjoyed their glow as I wrapped presents and thought of each of my children, their wives, and my grandchildren. Christmas came and went in a blur. I spent a week with eleven people besides me—six adults and five children. We shared a happy, hectic, laughing time, with sentences that started with "Remember when…" It ended too quickly as one by one, each son and his family returned to his own home, in New York, Maryland, or Tennessee.

I left the tree up for three weeks after Christmas. I told myself it was so beautiful I didn't want to take it down. The truth is, when I pack the ornaments away, I know my family will not return here to celebrate and fill my house with their noise and laughter for three years, as we meet one year in Maryland and one in New York.

The house reverted to quiet, the silence drowned out the laughter. I felt numb, not with fatigue but with loneliness. I am accustomed to being alone, and I enjoy solitude, but after spending time with my family the house feels like a hollow shell, with its tasty filling sucked out and devoured. I know I won't see them for months. My painful thoughts could leak out, like an imperceptible hole that allows a tire to go flat; they will taint each day if I allow it.

I removed the lights, coiled them neatly, and packed them in my Christmas box. I took all the ornaments from the tree and put each one into its cardboard home until next year.

I touch the glass birds that once nested in my Christmas tree and experience a fleeting longing for another place and for people no longer here. I hold the heart-shaped ornament with Adam's picture, then tuck it away in the box. I whisper words of gratitude for the days my house swelled with joy and family, I smile, and let a few tears fall.

Choices

The sun stretches its arms across the wall opposite me, capturing the painting of the Prudence Island Lighthouse with its morning reach. I imagine the real one, bathed in morning light, as clearly as this one on the wall. These winter days the sun rises farther south and appears almost behind my chair. I crane my neck far to the right to see it climb through the trees. In summer, it rises closer to due east and shines on my face as I sit and write. I could move to another spot this morning and soak in a warm sunbeam, but I chose to stay where I am and wake to my Prudence Island view.

I write every day for the joy of it. I love to follow the trail of my mind that goes in unexpected directions, and yet my book waits in my computer, hovering with anticipation. What keeps me from plunging in, reading, rewriting, making sense of the whole? Fear of failure? Fear that I won't get it right? Fear that no one will read it?

I use the excuse of time; it nips at my heels like an annoying dog—I don't have enough, I need long stretches, I'm waiting for more. As a mother of three small boys, I had many chores to do. Instead of putting my children off, and asking them to wait, which led to impatience and cranky outbursts, I sat down and played a game or built a block tower first. Then I went and attacked my tasks, leaving the boys happily on their own for a while.

I tell myself to let go of the witch of no time. I can take the time, it's there, lurking between loads of laundry and dirty dishes. It keeps me company as I ride my bike, lingers in my mind when I drive. The music of time winds through my legs, purrs at my heels, and begs for a few minutes. Listen to the story that wants to be told.

Some days I sit to write, and an unexpected story flows from my pen, a poem appears in my prose, words that might someday circle around and join hands to be a book, dance in my head. Thoughts call to me as I walk, and I fill my recorder, moment by moment, step-by-step.

The year ahead faces me, a blank canvas waiting to be filled. I am finished with the holiday hustle. I can pace my household chores, walk, and write. I can steal time from every day to work on my book, get lost in the stories and find my way to the end. I can sew on the missing button, mend the jeans and patch the holes. I can add a flourish or two, perhaps a piece of lace, until the finished product appears seamless, though imperfections will make it real. I can allow them to stay and tell my story the way it beats in my head. I know what I want, but I have to choose what to let go, make peace with what I can't have, and be grateful for what I do. My life is not a story easily written, but still I can choose—stay where I am, or walk forward, into the unknown.

My Lemon Tree

My lemon tree lives in my bright sunroom, cozy by day and quite chilly at night, and has adapted to being inside, though it flourishes when it moves to its outside home in late spring. No matter where it sits, it continues to provide sustenance for my eyes and nourishment for my soul. The creamy blooms look like the finest porcelain and the scent draws me to them.

I bought this lemon tree as a tiny twig many years ago, and it has grown as tall as I am, its height slightly curtailed by my recent pruning. I sit in my writing chair beside it, and the intoxicating fragrance fills my nose. Pink tinges the buds and the white blossoms which bloom for weeks. At the same time, lemons in various stages of ripeness hang scattered on the branches—a cluster of three yellow ones almost ready to be picked, a pair of lime green ones weeks away from harvesting, and here and there a single lemon, gradually turning yellow like the Goldfinches in the spring.

Its blossoms continue to appear when the fruits of its labor ripen. It does not focus on one thing at a time; the buds don't open all at once and then fall to the ground in a depleted white carpet like the magnolia. The fruit does not come exclusively in one season and then leave behind idle branches, bare of leaf or blossom. The dark green leaves hold their glossy shine year-round. Some years it produces over thirty tart, juicy fruits, while other years only a few lemons appear.

White buds, sprinkled generously over the limbs, swell with each passing day. I press my face into its green arms, avoiding the prickly long thorns that protect it. Stress disappears; I relax and float on the aroma of lemon blossoms.

I study the lemon tree and I am grateful for its lesson. It shares the beauty of its shiny leaves and exquisite waxy, white blooms. Its past effort to yield a crop of lemons does not prevent it from producing more blooms to add beauty to the world. I want to be like the lemon tree. Some years it bears fruit and some years it channels its energy into blossoming and laying the groundwork for a future harvest. It can take me years to lay the groundwork of writing and editing, before the fruit of a published book, but even then, I have other gifts to give. I wonder, *What gifts have I been given to share?* I love harvesting the lemons, finding and trying recipes, then sharing them for friends to enjoy. I also love harvesting words, and hope they bring sustenance and enjoyment too.

I am grateful for my lemon tree, and I am grateful for me. We all have years of stillness and years of growth, and the lemon tree reminds me that life is filled with both. When the fruit passes and new buds begin, they need time and care to produce fruit again.

Where I Wander

The song "The Wanderer" streams in my head this morning. The words and music popped into my brain, a jack-in-the-box released without warning. I can't remember any other words except those, but they float in time to the music, and they sing in the voice of the original performer, Dion, from 1961.

Why did I suddenly think of that song as I sit here quietly, stationary in my writing chair? I don't know, but I am a wanderer, and right now I wander through this decade of my life trying to figure it out, trying to figure *me* out. How did I get where I am? What successes and failures brought me here? What hurts have colored my view of the world?

We all carry wounds, some more disguised than others. We hide them like a smuggler crossing the border, and though no one else sees them, knowing that they exist can make our heart pound—in fear or anger. They can ache and fester with no apparent cure.

Old wounds reveal themselves in strange ways and can harden us and sometimes make it difficult to show love or tenderness. I wonder what wounds people carry when they are impatient, critical, or judgmental. Do they carry the wounds of criticism or indifference? Do they carry the wounds of harsh treatment and lash out when they feel threatened, afraid of being hurt again?

Where we have been and how rough the road we traveled influences who we become. Age changes our perception of life too. At twenty, often we think we will live forever. Death doesn't haunt our thoughts, nor does it when we turn thirty, forty, or even fifty. At sixty a glimmer of realization flickers. Although we may have many years left on this earth, we won't live for eternity. I turned a corner at seventy, and awareness began to settle in my mind, and more importantly, in my heart and soul. The world offers reminders everywhere that life doesn't last forever, and I provide my own—I tire more easily than I used to, I can't work in the yard for eight hours straight anymore.

Life circumstances led us in certain directions, as did the decisions we made. I walked paths I would like to change, but they have worn deep crevices within or molded to me, and I struggle to step out of them. I find myself retreating to the safety of the known and familiar, even though I want to take the challenging route; if I follow it in my writing, maybe it will help someone else to follow a different path too. Maybe they won't feel alone in the place they find themselves.

I want to go farther into the woods where the carpet of wildflowers grows, a spot that would have gone unnoticed if I had not followed the trail a little longer. I discover new things as I walk deeper into the forest of feelings and emotions. I want to acknowledge old wounds that hold me back and heal myself, and maybe someone else too.

I watch my grandchildren turn from babies to toddlers,

boys to men. How does it happen? In my mind, I am the same age, still thirty-nine and holding, like Jack Benny. Some days I feel overwhelmed by the care my yard requires, and I wonder if the time has come to sell my house. Then I wonder, *Where will I go?* I don't want to wander anywhere, except where I have been for the last forty-five years, right here.

Can You See?

What do you see when you look at me?
Do you see a body less fit and trim,
Or can you see the girl that still lives within?
Do you see the legs that sprint no more,
Or can you feel the spirit that still longs to soar?
Do you see the hands now spotted with age,
Or can you see the person who's still part of life's page?
A mother whose chicks have flown away,
Who writes to find purpose in every day,
To create a story that will last,
Touch a soul, remember the past.
The lawn looks mown for only a day,
But a word once written forever stays.
I tell my story through ink on the page,
When I am ninety, my mind won't be that age.
It will still run and ride a bike,
Cook dinner in evening's fading light.
It will still hold hands with someone small,
And long to be loved most of all.
It will still yearn for a warm, tender touch,
And want to be needed, when nothing is left but dust.

January Gift

❦

The present was not packed in a box or delivered by mail. It wasn't wrapped in fancy paper or tied with a ribbon, but it was cloaked in shades of vivid blue and rusty red, and it arrived at precisely 1:48 p.m. on January 20. In the midst of a snowstorm, I looked out my sunporch window and saw four chubby Bluebirds sitting in the lilac bush. That day an icy wind howled and the temperature hovered in the single digits; the round blue puffballs tried to capture every bit of warmth they could find. I was convinced they had been blown off course or sought shelter in that winter storm, because I had never seen Bluebirds at my Chepachet home.

The following year, January 20 was a day as different as winter and spring. The temperature reached a balmy thirty-eight degrees beneath a cloudless blue sky, and although a gentle breeze swayed through the trees, it didn't deter me from my afternoon walk. As I prepared to leave, I glanced out the sunporch window, and there once again in the lilac bush sat four brilliant Bluebirds. Not another bird inhabiting this part of New England sports this vibrant color. The tawny red encircling its breast accents the bright blue feathers on its back. Two pairs lingered outside, the females a slightly subdued version of the males, but still that distinct and incredible blue.

I consider Bluebirds a gift, and welcome guests in my yard, in part because they visit so rarely, but also because they remind me of summer days at my childhood home on Prudence Island, Rhode Island. Back then Bluebirds were plentiful in the island's open fields. Although they don't like to make their home in the woodsy environment where I now live, they don't mind dropping by for a winter snack.

The four that came to the feeders that January day provided a delightful surprise, and I hoped they would return for several days or even weeks as they did the year before. If I saw them again it wouldn't matter whether the sun was shining or the snow was swirling, because their cheery call would be a reminder that spring would soon be here. Little did I know when that thought flitted through my mind that one week later when I saw the Bluebirds, we would be in the midst of a blizzard that would leave behind over two feet of drifted snow—the first of many snowstorms the Bluebirds and I would endure before spring finally did come again.

Blizzard

I watch the snow and think about other storms when big soft flakes floated from the sky, caressed my cheeks, and muted the noise of the world. Silence surrounded me; when I stopped shoveling and listened, I heard nothing but the sound of my breath and the whisper of falling snow. I love walking in that hushed world. I stroll down a nearby side street in my special snow sneakers, and I deem those days a gift, but not today.

Today, the snow and wind rage, heaving their angry voices at anything in their path. The wind circles, howling and planning its attack. It drives the fine snow through the screens enclosing the porch and coats the floor. From my sunroom windows I see sheets of white fly by outside. The mounting snow forms drifts along the stone walls and against the car. The temperature drops as daylight emerges, and the rising sun brings no warmth.

Flashes of color dash by the window. The Cardinals and Bluebirds startle the snow with their brilliance. The birds descend on the feeders like humans converging on the grocery store for bread and milk. They form a taxi service to the seed port; one lands to have a snack, and the next waits in the lilac bush to take his turn when a spot opens.

I need to shovel, but I know as fast as I shovel more snow will fall. I used to prefer waiting until the storm finished hurling snow and moved on, but in recent years, I've decided frequent small stints of shoveling make more sense for my body and back. Today the wind makes me question that wisdom, but I eat breakfast and then face the baying animal with a shovel as my lone defense.

The snow comes with such force that my shovel can't keep pace. By the time I clear around my car, push the snow from it, then remove that, another two inches fall. I move on to the driveway and continue my counterattack. The wind charges through the trees, flinging the snow against my face in a stinging spray. I have chemical hand warmers in my mittens and two layers of clothes under my snow pants, three under my jacket. I wear a ski mask over my face and my purple wool hat on my head. I move slowly, shoveling for the long haul, not a quick sprint.

An hour later I take a break, and after a warming cup of coffee, I repeat my car clearing and shovel my half-moon driveway in the opposite direction. By then, my front steps have accumulated two more inches of new snow, though I swept them clean when I came out. Even shoveling in stages, my arms and back ache as I go through the motions again and again, and I grow weary faster. Why don't I hire someone to do this job? Because despite my sore back, I know when I finish, I will feel a sense of accomplishment and self-reliance. But this storm threatens to overwhelm me, and I wonder if I can defeat it.

The wind and snow intensity reach the promised afternoon peak. Even my sunroom feels dark and gloomy;

snow covers all the windows and blocks the light. The birds move in a frantic, shadowy dance outside the frosted panes. The temperature continues to fall, the wind moans, and I hear the trees creaking and the gunshot report of a snapping branch. The unsettling sound makes me decide to stay inside a little longer, even though it means removing eight inches of white from my car yet again.

I eventually return to the task of eliminating the most recent round of snow. I would prefer to stay inside by the fire, but if I don't clear it now, my car will become an igloo, and I'll be trapped. I might not want to drive anywhere, but I will feel safer knowing I can leave my driveway if I need to unexpectedly. When my tired arms can't lift one more shovelful, I hear a grating sound. A passing truck with a plow scrapes the heavy snow left by the town plows from both ends of my drive. The unexpected help lifts my spirits and on a final surge of energy, I finish.

The next morning the world wakes white and sparkling. Wind sways the treetops and like distant wind chimes, twigs snap and whine. The temperature remains frigid despite the sun; it can't penetrate the cold and sub-zero windchill. No snowy walks for me today. I'll sit by the fire, read a book, and rest—tucked in until the world thaws.

I Think I Will Remember, But...

I glimpse long-ago memories that haunt me. Things I thought I would remember in detail, but don't. They hide like a hologram that won't quite take shape—a quivering mass of glowing particles. Why can't I form them into something real?

I planned to keep a baby book for each of my children, but it didn't turn out that way. I had one for Eric, my firstborn, in which I wrote his name, birthdate, and weight. For baby two, Peter, I had a baby book in which I wrote—nothing. By the time Adam, my third child came along, I didn't even have a baby book. I convinced myself that I would remember special events for each of them—the bumps and bruises, the mountains they climbed, and their achievements along the way. I would remember their first words, when they took their first steps, the funny and profound things they said, and when they started to read—but I don't.

Occasionally a memory flutters by to taunt me, but like trying to catch a rainbow, it slips through my fingers and disappears. I'm sure they lurk hidden behind a door in my brain as clearly as my own childhood memories, I just haven't found the key to open it yet.

I cannot see any logic or pattern to what I remember.

When I wrote *The Ferry Home*, I remembered events from my childhood as if they had happened yesterday. I didn't even know I remembered them until I started writing. If I kept writing from where the memories ended when I left Prudence, could I fill in all the blanks until I began to write in 2013? What would jog my memory? Why does it matter? Because I want to feel again my mother's hand on my shoulder as she walked by the kitchen table where I sat, my head bent over my schoolbook. Without a word, her gentle encouragement in that touch assured me that all was well.

I still have my parents' bedroom set. Following my mother's death nineteen years ago, the scent that floated out when I pulled on the drawer handles stabbed a knife of pain deep inside me and triggered my tears. That familiar aroma, so tangible, but the person it belonged to no longer here. I try to connect it to happy memories, but I still miss her, and her fragrance reminds me of that. I carry smells with me, deep in my being, and even today, many years later, I can sense her, smell her, when I open those drawers.

My grandmother's stories live in the distance too. I want to remember more of my parents and grandmother than the postcard-size images contained in my memoir. I want manuscript-size memories for each of them. How did she meet my grandfather? What was it like growing up on Block Island? What activities did she enjoy as a girl? The answers shimmer on the fringes of my mind. I want to recover them. Can I find them if I follow the secret path? Their disappearance reminds me to write the words, write the stories now, so the page can keep them safe before they vanish.

Soup Days

The wind has begun its freight train journey through my yard and I know snow, though not yet visible, rides on the caboose. The sky remains the gray of early morning, before the sun breaks the horizon. Usually my sunroom resembles a lamp on a dimmer switch. The glowing light grows brighter and brighter as the day wakens, and the sun peeks through the windows, creeping through the trees and over the stone wall. Today the world hasn't grown any lighter since seven o'clock; the switch is stuck and the sky stays dark with unfallen snow.

I love snowy days, they inspire me to make soup. I think about butternut squash with ginger and Armenian lentil. I have made minor adjustments to the squash recipe, resulting in a thick, creamy, golden purée with a kick of ginger and a velvety smoothness from the addition of sweet potatoes. I regard it as my healing soup. If a friend becomes ill, I take her this soup. If someone dies, I take it to the family. Soups sustain me in the winter. If I have company for supper, I make soup.

I haven't made the Armenian lentil soup for a while, but I made a few additions to that recipe as well—cook the spices with the sautéed onions, add a glug of red wine and a sweet potato. Delicious, and it fills the house with the fragrance of cinnamon, clove, and coriander—warm, comforting smells for a winter day.

Snowy days soften the sharp edges, muffle sounds, and frost the tree limbs. The rocks that build the stone walls around my yard, run together under a ribbon of white. I can sit in my sunroom and the quiet surrounds me, like I've crawled inside an igloo, except I can still see the birds. They arrive frenetically on snowy days and can't seem to eat fast enough.

My neighbor scrapes the snow from the edge of his driveway with a shovel, then starts his snowblower, and noise intrudes into my quiet white space. I want to creep inside myself and explore my snowy brain. Will it stay quiet and muffled too? Or will the storm release it to go exploring through the snow-covered woods of my mind? Or maybe I will spend the day making soup.

More Than a Meal

I love good food. I enjoy eating it and preparing it. Food alone doesn't make a meal special; the circumstances and the people who eat with us make it memorable. Sometimes the place, or the events leading to the meal imprint it in our mind; seldom can the food alone accomplish this.

My family occasionally ordered Chinese food takeout, from a restaurant called BingSum, when I was growing up. It came in white cardboard containers packed in a brown paper bag. If I was lucky enough to go with my dad to collect it, I inhaled the aroma of sweet torment all the way home, as my stomach growled in anticipation.

When I was about thirteen, one of my father's friends had flooded an area behind his store to make a small ice rink. His son and a friend, both accomplished skaters, took turns partnering with my sister and me. I had never become a proficient skater, because my hands and feet always got too cold too fast, and I would have to stop, but with one of their arms on my waist and a hand holding mine, I skated without falling for the whole afternoon. This time my hands and feet stayed warm.

Exhilaration consumed me as I glided over the ice, round and round the homemade rink, with a handsome young man beside me. Sometimes all we need in life to feel confident instead of frightened is a hand to hold. The taller boy gradually shifted to skating more with me, and of course I fell in love. I imagined seeing him for another skating session, when he alone would be my partner. That never happened. I never saw him again, but my imagination stayed in high gear for weeks.

After several hours of skating in the fresh, cold air, my appetite shifted into high gear as well. We finally said goodbye and drove back home, stopping along the way at Bing Sum. We ordered our usual meal: chop suey, chow mein, white rice, Chinese noodles, and almond cookies, but that night, as my family gathered in the kitchen, it was the most delicious food I had ever tasted.

Moments

*E*very day starts the same way when I am home, and yet, each day holds moments unique to itself. If I move blindly through my routine, I easily miss them. The light comes in my bedroom window and dances unfelt over my face, and yet, my eyes open to its brightness. The rich aroma of coffee brewing travels up the stairs, wanders to my brain, and I breathe its welcome 'good morning' greeting as I stretch away sleepy stiffness.

Cherished moments make life alive. They give meaning to the day, holding it gently, with care and tenderness, like cradling a baby bird. Ignoring moments jumbles them together, crushes them into a ball like a wad of old love letters headed for the trash, each one indistinguishable from the next.

Today the sun glints off the snow as I sit in my writing chair; I drink my coffee and enjoy its vanilla fragrance and warming touch. The inside chilliness reflects the outside temperature of ten degrees, and I wrap my hands around the mug to warm them, while I wait for the sizzle and hiss that signals the heat soon to come from the radiator. The sun highlights the picture of the Prudence Island Lighthouse that hangs on my wall, opposite where I sit. If I'm distracted, or oblivious, I will miss the fleeting spotlight.

I smile as this picture of the place I love glimmers before my eyes, beckoning me to plan a day there soon. My grandson painted it for me as a Christmas gift. I imagine his face and his smile.

Moments, easily lost, easily overlooked in mindless routine, but each a gift to begin the day. The light changes with the season as the sun creeps through the sky, not only rising earlier, but also in a slightly different place. By summer, its light will glint through the leaves directly behind my house. Today it angles in through the corner and kisses the memory of Prudence.

Outside, the feeders sit empty, though I heard the call of the Red-bellied Woodpecker. Then I see a squirrel feasting on the suet. He eats his fill for the moment and moves on. I know I will see songbirds if I sit a little longer. A Downy Woodpecker lands on the suet vacated by the recent furry, gray mass. Today's cold doesn't trigger the feeding frenzy of snowy days. The birds take their time before going out for coffee, and I wait patiently, sipping mine.

Coffee and Bluebirds

I gazed upon a white world—the ground coated in snow, the trees encased in dripping ice that soon will puddle and be gone. Right before it snows, the earth exudes the smell of cold and gray. They press back, like granite, as I walk, and I breathe the still unseen snow above and around me. Yesterday when I walked, I wore scarves wrapped around my neck, and mittens and gloves layered over my hands. The coming snow hung heavy in the air, and frosty needles stung my nose.

A flash of blue landed on the tree above me—a Bluebird. They usually come when it snows, traveling in groups, four or six at one time, always in pairs. Brilliant blue calls attention to them, and even though they aren't purposely hiding, I'm always amazed when I see them. Sometimes I start my day, coffee cup in hand, waiting for their arrival at the feeders outside my window. When I see them, round, roly-poly little birds with friendly faces, my spirits lift.

I didn't see them early this morning, and I worried that they had moved on. I drank my coffee, ate my breakfast, got dressed, made the bed, still nothing. I gave up. Later, as I heated my second cup of coffee, I glanced out the window, and to my delight, two Bluebirds sat on a small branch near the suet feeder. The males, with their backs to the window, showed off their brilliant blue plumage. I couldn't see the russet and white of their breasts and bellies, but I knew it existed, and it made the blue even brighter in my mind.

The feeders hang close to my windows, nestled in the L formed by the kitchen and sunroom. I can stand in either room and see them clearly. I enjoy watching all the birds that stop by, but whenever Bluebirds arrive, I abandon my tasks and reach for my camera. A pair lands on the same suet feeder, but neither seems to mind; in tandem they peacefully peck at the fatty mixture. Six arrive, three males and three females.

"I'm so glad to see you again. I hope you'll stay longer this time, you're so beautiful." I am captivated by Bluebirds. I cannot see one without smiling, like a child when he catches sight of the merry-go-round at the park. The flying horses bring light to his eyes and a smile of anticipation to his face—a look of pure joy. If I became a bird, I would want them for my friends. Does the incredible shade of blue set them apart? Or their black-eyed friendly expressions? I don't know, but I have an unconscious attachment to Bluebirds because they lived on Prudence Island when I lived there as a child. I keep taking pictures, and I know that when my heart feels heavy with longing, I find respite in a flash of blue, and when I see a Bluebird, I am home.

Radiators

This morning I slept later than usual, and when I rose, a special February light glowed through the windows, a brilliance that radiates from a snow-covered world. It reflects a unique luminosity and holds the house close in its hands. I stand at the top of the stairs and absorb it. I can see the view out three of the bedrooms from my spot. That ethereal white light serves as the first indication of the arrival of snow in the night. It doesn't happen with a dusting, but today sixteen inches of smooth, undisturbed white blankets the ground. The carpeted road softens the noise of cars driving by. I love the peacefulness of snow; I feel cocooned and cushioned by quiet. It holds the world at bay.

I tiptoe downstairs, feeling the hush surround me. I listen to the chorus in my living room, a steady whistle in one corner, a high-pitched wavering in another, and a baritone hiss from the farthest nook. Beneath it all, the furnace rumbles its bass vibrato from the cellar. I listen to the radiators and it carries me back through the years like a time warp. They heated the home where I lived as a child. They quickly warm the space around them, but their real charm can be found in their friendly sounds.

One radiator sizzles like bacon in a pan, and in the background a quiet crackle sounds. Two radiators in the room play a duet. It starts pianissimo, and builds to forte, then gradually backs off again. Finally, it fades, like a ship sailing away, growing smaller and smaller. I hear a faint lingering whistle from the other end of the room, mournful, the last attempt at song before silence.

My two-hundred-year-old farmhouse contains one heating zone. When I get up in the morning, I give the thermostat a gentle nudge, and within five minutes I can enjoy my coffee in comfortable warmth, surrounded by a chorus of radiator songs. On cold damp days when I'm alone, the sound of the radiator keeps me company. Unlike the methods of heat production designed by modern technology, radiators sing and chatter. They provide not only heat, but also cheery companionship. They whistle and tap while the steam escapes, then the tune changes as they flow into the rhythm of creating heat.

As a child I'd climb out of the bathtub on a cold night and slip into radiator-warmed pajamas, safe and cozy as I headed to bed. I still warm my pajamas and towel on the radiator, and step from the tub into the luxury of a heated towel, then I slide into sleep wrapped in a blanket of warmth.

New houses today do not include radiators, a loss to the march of progress. They're heavy and hard to move, I know. I have struggled with more than one when I painted a room, or replaced the carpet, but to me they are worth the effort. This generation and succeeding ones will miss the comforting atmosphere they provide. Summer offers the background music of crickets and songbirds, but in winter, I curl up with a book surrounded by the music of the radiators. On a snowy New England morning that snaps with brittle cold, they warm my body and soul, and they sing!

Winter Music

Whistle, clank, hiss, sizzle,
Singing soprano tunes.
Bass vibrato rumbles low,
'Neath my feet and through my bones.
Staccato taps in greeting,
Cheerful noises fill the room.
Overhead five paper loons
Glide on steamy, heated air,
They fly in endless circles,
Content to go nowhere.
The chorus now crescendos,
My soul and toes are warm,
Music slowly fades away,
The Radiator's Song.

Fickle February

The air touches my face springtime soft as I walk this late February morning. The temperature has already reached fifty-five degrees, and the fecund smell of spring surrounds me. The grass in the front yard sprouts green, and tiny snowdrops, the first harbingers of spring, bloom in the garden. The birds sing their springtime songs too. The Cardinals call, two whistles followed by five chirps, and ask their neighbors about the latest gossip. A Flicker rat-a-tat-tats a message to relay the recent news.

February arrives as fickle and undependable as a lover on Valentine's Day. Sometimes it holds your hand and brings you flowers, and sometimes it comes disguised as April, then slaps you in the face with endless record-breaking cold. We've had a windchill of minus twenty-three one day, and two weeks later, warmth of over sixty degrees. A few years ago, February delivered relentless snow. Storms arrived in wave after wave. The snow piled so high around my driveway I had to shovel the top off the mounds to make room for the next storm to land. My parents bought this house almost sixty years ago, and for the first time, ice dams formed and caused the roof to leak. I didn't see the snowdrops until mid-April. But everything thrived; growing things slept through it all, snuggled beneath their deep snow blanket that kept them warm and fed them through the icy winter days. The plants knew enough to stay put until true spring arrived, when they emerged rested and refreshed.

February in New England should be cold. Seventy degrees—how can that be real? April has usurped February. This delights many people, but I think it disrupts the order of things. It confuses the plants, the birds, and our bodies. If seventy degrees lasts longer than a minute in February, it pokes at the plants, waking them before they finish sleeping and drawing them out into the morning air. They release delicate shoots, and the cold that always follows freezes tender growth and cuts them off at their feet. One year, warm winter days like this, with no snow cover, enticed daffodils and shrubs from hibernation. Then, a late spring blizzard and freezing temperatures left them shriveled and lifeless. It completely destroyed the Rhode Island peach crop.

This year might play out as a repeat of that tempting warmth. My blueberry bushes have already budded, which doesn't bode well for the crop this year. As a gardener, I know frost and frigid winds will still pursue us, and I'm afraid those buds will never blossom and bear fruit. When I return to my yard, I stroll around my small front garden, encircled by a lattice fence. The daffodils have already sent up green shoots. The strong hand of temptation pulls on me to clear away the winter rubble and cut back the dead stalks. However, although the weather whispers April, and makes me yearn for spring, the calendar still shows February. I will remain patient and wait.

Will It Matter?

I'm sitting in my sunroom listening to the rain. It comes in waves, sometimes gently dancing on the skylight and sometimes sounding like an army marching overhead, drumming to the beat of its feet. I want to close my eyes and hear the rise and fall of sound led by an unseen conductor, pooling in puddles in my mind. I could sit here all day listening, carried away on the tide to the recesses of my brain, where niggling questions live…

How will my writing read in a hundred years? Or even ten? Does what I write make a difference? Does it touch the reader? I write of things that matter to me: friendship, love, illness, loss, and grief, but also joy, and passing moments that touch me. They all affect every life, but sometimes we get too enmeshed in busyness to think about or acknowledge how they make us feel.

I write to capture the tiny details that might go unnoticed, the things in life that build faith and help us deal with loss as the days flow one to another, and things change, but stay the same. How many of us take an extra deep breath on the first warm day of spring and never stop to think why, or recognize how the air feels different? Do those moments change us too?

We all exist in the cycle of changing seasons: seeds

get sown, plants grow, then die to be reborn in the spring, or sometimes not. When I feel connected to the world outside, and its variations through the seasons, it gives depth and breadth to my life. Without it I skim over the top, adrift, without roots.

I write about changes in the feel and smell of the wind and the sounds of the birds, from November to August. Even transformation has a sameness to it. I scatter a handful of tiny seeds over a pot of soil each spring and have faith that I will soon harvest pungent basil for summer salads. Winter brings loss. The leaves dry and fall to the ground, the garden sleeps in its brown bedraggled sleeping bag, and then spring throws a bright, calico quilt across the earth.

These changes reflect life. They matter and weave us together into a human tapestry. Friends and family become ill or grow old and die. New babies come into the world. The cycle continues, the latter brings joy, the former pain and struggle. I love going into my garden every day in the spring to see what new flowers have bloomed, but I am sad when the last daffodil shrivels and dies until next year. I keep hoping that as I go through the cycle again, and again, the rhythm will become part of me, and I will accept loss more easily. Children grow and leave home. If I had written more about them as little boys, could I recapture their special essence now? The smell of their just-washed curls, or the feel of their silky cheeks and chubby hands in mine?

I am a channel. I write the words I have been given. I write about life's truths: we all feel pain, we all hate to see it felt by someone we love. Sometimes hard things get better, and sometimes, they don't.

Solitude Shoes

Currents of change flowed over the world in recent years, bringing troubled and uncertain times, and no life went unaffected. I lived in social isolation, with Silence as my roommate, and although I learned to accept its presence, I found the cloud of uncertainty that filled my silence unsettling. It irritated my mind like poison ivy irritates my body. I couldn't focus on anything. I wandered from task to task, leaving each one unfinished.

I couldn't travel to see my family, who all live out of state, and like most people, I visited a few friends from afar. I didn't share dinner and a game with them, only a distant stroll. Shopping became an emotional challenge as well as a physical one. And yet, I considered myself fortunate; I had a safe place to live and all I needed to survive. I could contact my family and see them on a video call. I had flowers growing around me, and I could go outside and walk, or work in my garden, which quieted my mind. If I didn't listen to the radio or the news on TV, I could settle into the comfort of normalcy for a while, and convince myself that life hadn't changed. I allowed the sounds of radiators sizzling, the birds singing, or rain falling to be the background to my life.

For some, I'm sure, the unfamiliar solitude felt like

wearing a pair of uncomfortable shoes—not only spike heels and pointy toes, but also two sizes too small. They chafed and pinched and rubbed blisters on their souls, and they lived in constant pain. Though old and worn, my shoes have molded to my feet over the years. I have lived my whole life, or most of it, in my solitude shoes. I wore them often as a child, because I lived on a small island with no playmates nearby except my sister, Pat, and I often played by myself. As a teenager I took those shoes out now and then and sank into their familiar feel, when I needed to think, or I found myself without plans on a Friday night. I wore them when I rode my bike around the back streets of my neighborhood, or took long walks.

Even when I got married the shoes came with me. I wore them when my husband worked late, or when he traveled and I stayed home with young children. Sometimes a pebble snuck in and a sore spot developed, until I could dislodge the culprit or take off the shoes. I went through a divorce and my children grew up and left home. I wore my shoes most of the time and dislodged a constant flow of pebbles. I learned not to wait, to dump them out right away, and continue my walk, focused on the relief of no pebbles. Sometimes the shoes stayed in my closet for days and weeks at a time; then I longed for their comfort, for the squishy unbinding feel of them. I reached for the shoes and sighed in relief as my feet melted into them.

I have worn my solitude shoes almost every day the past few years, and the soles have thinned. They developed worn spots that allow the pebbles of loneliness to enter more frequently; sometimes I don't empty them right away and the pain travels directly to my soul. But I know people around the world wear their own shoes, and I am the lucky one, because my shoes fit my feet. I have worn their solitude for so long, I have grown accustomed to it. I empty the pebbles, work in my garden, and keep going.

Promise Song

Solitude cries into the night
Like the call of a distant loon,
Morning wakes, yawning its light,
And the daffodils still bloom.

Winter lingers without care,
Raindrops drum an angry tune.
North winds leave the branches bare,
But the daffodils still bloom.

Weeds of worry choke the view
Of more healing days to come,
Lilacs scent the softening air,
And the daffodils still bloom.

Empty places fill the pews,
Prayers are said in separate rooms,
Thoughtful hands reach out to share,
And the daffodils still bloom.

Sunshine soothes the troubled soul
When pain and sorrow loom,
Love is sent from far away,
And the daffodils still bloom.

The porch swing creaks a promise song,
Someone will sit beside me soon,
Fireflies blink the end of day,
And the daffodils always bloom.

Recipes

Butternut Squash Soup

1 medium butternut squash, cut in half lengthwise,
   seeds removed
2 tablespoons olive oil
1 medium onion, coarsely chopped
1 piece fresh ginger (2½ inches long and ¾ inch thick),
   peeled and chopped
2 medium carrots, peeled and chopped
4-5 cups vegetable broth
1 medium sweet potato, peeled and cut into 1/2 inch cubes
1 12 oz can evaporated skim milk
1-2 teaspoons salt, to taste
½ teaspoon nutmeg
½ teaspoon black pepper

1. Heat oven to 425 °F.
2. Place squash cut side up in a 9x13 inch pan. Add ½
   inch water to bottom of pan, cover with foil and bake
   until squash is tender, 40-50 minutes.
3. Heat olive oil in Dutch oven, add onion and sauté
   until translucent. Add ginger and carrots, sauté another 5 minutes, stirring occasionally.

4. Add broth and sweet potatoes. Scoop cooked squash out of skin, and add.
5. Bring to a boil, cover, reduce heat and simmer until all veggies are tender, about 45 minutes.
6. Process in batches in blender until smooth. (Don't fill blender more than half full with hot soup.)
7. Add evaporated milk, nutmeg, pepper, and salt to taste.
8. Serves 6-8

Holly Cakes

Base
1½ cups sifted flour
½ cup butter, room temperature
½ cup brown sugar, packed
1 teaspoon baking powder
⅛ teaspoon salt

Topping
2 egg whites, room temperature
 pinch salt
½ cup brown sugar, packed
½ cup chopped walnuts or pecans
½ teaspoon vanilla extract

1. Preheat oven to 350 °F.
2. Grease 9 inch square pan, line with parchment paper and grease again. Allow paper to extend up sides of the pan to make removal of cookies easier.
3. Make Base: Cream butter and brown sugar until smooth.
4. Mix in flour, baking powder and salt. Mixture will be crumbly.
5. Press into prepared pan.
6. Make Topping: Beat egg whites with salt until foamy and white, gradually beat in brown sugar, beat until peaks form.
7. Fold in vanilla and chopped nuts.
8. Spread topping evenly over base.
9. Bake about 25-30 minutes, or until meringue is no

longer sticky on top, and a tooth pick pressed all the way through base comes out clean.

10. Cool completely on wire rack before removing from pan and cutting into bars.

11. Makes 24.

Acknowledgements

Over the Garden Wall grew from a tiny idea seed, but it took six years for it to reach maturity. The pandemic both slowed its progress and motivated me to finish, as it renewed my appreciation for moments that matter. Writing is a solitary pursuit, but bringing a book to publication requires a community of support, and I am deeply grateful to mine; without you, *Over the Garden Wall* would have remained a dormant seed.

My thanks to the Harmony Writers Group, who listened to my stories and poems, made suggestions, and encouraged me to continue. I'm grateful to the staff at the Harmony Library who welcomed me for hours of rewriting and always provided a quiet corner for me to work.

Thank you, beta readers: Belle DeCosta, Bonnie Gold, Jane Loomis, Kristen Whelan, Barbara Whitman, and Mary Volk, for your time, insights, and enthusiastic support. Thank you, Barbara, for your talents transforming flower photos into sketch-like images.

My heartfelt gratitude to my editors: Dawn Alexander, whose guidance and expertise made my stories better, and copy editor Martha Reynolds, whose knowledge and attention to detail polished my prose. You both went beyond the minimum required and took time to answer all my questions.

My thanks to Dawn and Steven Porter and the staff at Stillwater River Publications for designing the cover and publishing my book.

To my friend Judy Little, thank you for generously sharing your Prudence Island home, where I continue to find inspiration as I watch the day begin and end beside the bay. My love and appreciation to my son Adam, who continues to encourage me to write.

With love and thanks to Sandy, for sixty-five years of friendship and for repeatedly saying, "You have to keep writing." This is for you.

Finally, to my readers, your thoughtful comments and emails are gifts that inspire me to keep writing. Thank you for choosing *Over the Garden Wall*. I hope you enjoy it and discover your own moments that matter.

 **Debbie Kaiman Tillinghast** is the author of *The Ferry Home*, a memoir; *A Dream Worth Keeping*, a novel; and *A Gift of Cookies, a Gift of Love*, a collection of cookie recipes and stories.

Her writing has appeared in *Country* magazine, and her poetry has been featured in nine anthologies published by the Association of Rhode Island Authors.

A retired teacher and nutrition educator, she now devotes her time to volunteering, gardening, walking, writing, and spending time with her family.

Visit her at www.debbiekaimantillinghast.com or www.facebook.com/debbiekaimantillinghast.

www.ingramcontent.com/pod-product-compliance
Lightning Source LLC
Chambersburg PA
CBHW051506260626
47162CB00008B/2849